love on the korlyan moon

petra palerno

contents

☆ Introduction   vii
☆ Trigger/Content Warnings   ix

1. A Higher Power, or Whatever   1
2. A Bitter Word   9
3. An Accident   17
4. No Better Than a Pup   29
5. Just a Little Guy   37
6. Strung Up   45
7. Playing Doctor   53
8. Good Boys   63
9. A Caring Gesture   69
10. Fingerpaints   75
11. A Great Honor   83
12. I Can't Promise You That   93
13. Splish Splash, It's an Alien Bath   101
14. Helping Hands   111
15. Blaster Barbeque   119
16. Keep Her or Die Trying   125
17. A Sniff Too Far   131
18. The Jewels   139
19. Picked Apart   149
20. More than Honorable   155
21. Burning for Me   161
22. Traditions   169
23. Brothers in Fate   175
24. Hide and Seek   181
25. No Antidote   191
26. My Destiny   197
27. Marked   203
28. First Timers   211
29. Second Timers   217
☆ Epilogue   223

☆ Glossary 229
☆The Bubble-verse 231

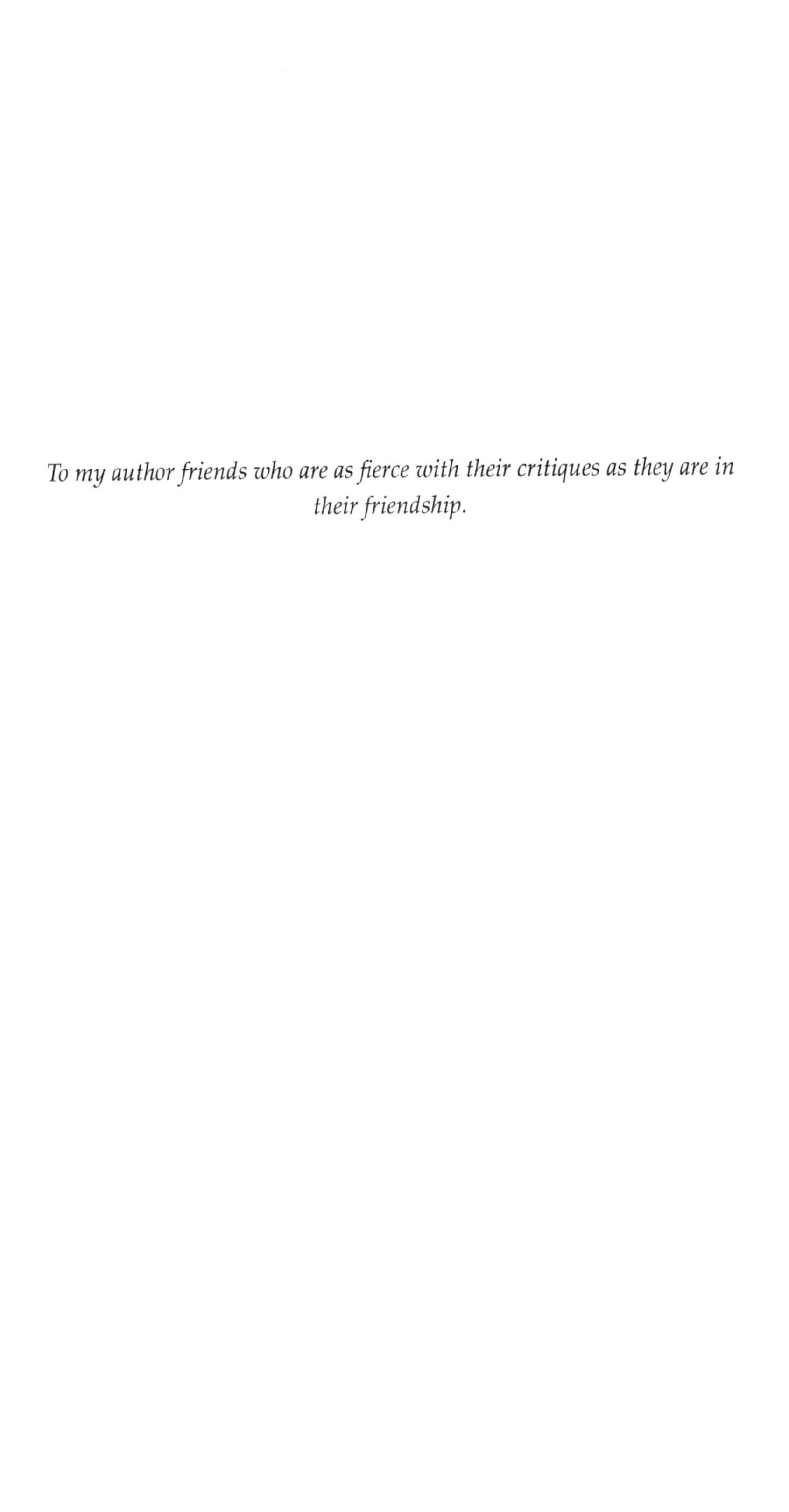

To my author friends who are as fierce with their critiques as they are in their friendship.

☆ introduction

Dear Reader,

The evil hive-minded Deenz alien have been abducting human women and forcing them to work as bubble dancers for extraterrestrial enjoyment. But when the prince of the planet Sontafrul 6 realizes his fated mate is one of those women, he declares war to liberate her kind. As the battle rages, the Deenz abandon their human cargo all over the galaxy. That's where Lena and Kitaico's story begins.

XOXO,
    PETRA PALERNO

PS: This story is intended as a standalone novel inside the Bubble Babes universe. There is no required reading before you embark on your trip to the Korlyan Moon.

☆ trigger/content warnings

As we prepare to embark on Kitaico and Lena's story, please keep in mind the following trigger and content warnings— mental health matters.

Alien abduction, fear of drowning, drowning discussed, human trafficking discussed, SA mentioned, forced heat, chaffing, needles, stinging, tattooing, fangs, poison, restraints, alien culture discussion on honor suicide, violence, dismemberment, kidnapping, tattooing, pregnancy (epilogue), xenophobia regarding humans, hand to hand combat, death, graphic sexual content including masturbation, oral, penetrative sex, tentacle sex, anal sex, and double penetration.

a higher power, or whatever

IF I HAD to choose someplace to die, this would be it.

Maybe I wouldn't have chosen the journey it took to get here —I'd happily skip the alien abduction and trafficking bit. But as I drift into a brightly-colored, unknown ocean, it's pretty damn peaceful.

I learned long ago that worrying about things out of my control was useless. I could rage, scream, and slam my fist into my plastic security bubble, but it won't make a difference.

I am going to die, and I'm going to wonder at the beauty of this place before I go. I doubt another human has seen these rainbow-hued fishlike creatures swimming by. A set of googly eyes dangle from long stalks below their torpedo-shaped bodies. Their scales glint in the sunlight as the schools float around me, almost reminding me of camera flashes back on Earth.

I take a deep breath and try to enjoy their unearthly elegance, leaning my back against the gently curving wall of my security pod.

This plastic bubble I've danced in has become familiar. I

know every scratch and ding. Despite how much you claw at its wall, it won't open from the inside.

Whatever space-age plastic the Deenz aliens use is robust. I don't know how much of the growing pressure it can handle as we descend further into the depths of this seemingly bottomless ocean.

The sunlight from the surface is ever waning, and the waters around me get darker and murkier the further I fall.

Another breath fills my chest as I try to quell the anxiety creeping in from the peripherals of my psyche. The school of creatures follows me like companions ushering me to the afterlife.

I put a hand against the plastic enclosure to thank them for not leaving me alone. I've always loved the ocean. Many of my tattoos are of underwater scenes: the coral reef on my calf, the stingray guarding my bicep, and my favorite tattoo—Aphrodite reclined on the half shell on my shoulder.

My soul has always been called to the water, so I guess this demise is fitting.

Thanks, universe, or whatever higher power controls this kind of thing.

As I try to project my gratitude to these little aquatic creatures and some higher power, I catch a flash of yellow from the corner of my eye. It moves too fast for me to get a good look. Spinning around in my bubble, I search for whatever it was.

As the school of alien fish shift suddenly to the left, I see him.

A muscular canary-yellow alien, his head full of pulsating tentacles, gapes at me. The tentacles shift as if moved by the underwater currents. They splay around his head like a lion's mane. His strong arms and legs pump as he descends with my bubble.

I say "he" because his cock is something you really can't miss. It isn't hard, but still floats proudly on display. His dick's impressive length is nestled in tentacles similar to the ones that surround his head, but they're much shorter. Almost like if you traded out pubes for a sea anemone. I guess that makes sense since his head "hair" is also comprised of tentacles.

I wonder what that would feel like. I quickly scrub the thought from my mind.

I'm more than likely going to die, and I don't want my last thoughts to be about alien dick.

I break my gaze from his crotch, not wanting to be a complete and total pervert. His smooth yellow skin is covered in a pattern of squiggly teal rings. He's got the physique of an Olympic swimmer, with a broad set of shoulders tapering into powerful legs.

His eyes are blue and bore into me as if questioning my very existence.

"Hi," I huff, taken aback by this strange alien Adonis who's found me.

When I speak, two of his head tentacles that appear longer than the rest spring out and grip the outside of my bubble. My descent stops so rapidly that I drop to my knees like a stone.

Tentacle Man pulls me closer. The strength in those two thick appendages sends a strange thrill through me. He puts his face against the plastic and appraises me with his full lips agape.

"What are you?" He cocks his head, his deep voice muffled through the water.

"I'm Lena. I'm human," I whisper, shocked he can speak.

He screws up his mouth and furrows his brows.

"I don't understand you," he says, tapping a spot in front of his ear. "I don't have a translator chip, and I don't think you speak Andjin. There's no tech allowed during the Great Proving —we are only as the goddess created us."

What in the flying fuck is the Great Proving?

But even in my confusion, I realized he's stopped my bubble from dropping further into the ocean...does this mean I won't die?

"Are you going to help me?" I say slowly, as if that might help him understand me.

"I'm sorry, I don't know your language. I don't even know what species you are…but it seems like you're in danger." His face softens, and he places his slightly webbed fingers against the glass.

"Can you understand me? If you can, nod," he tells me softly.

I nod, and he smiles.

"Well, at least one of us can get our point across…." He trails off as if catching sight of my body for the first time.

I'm wearing the thin, near-pornographic costume that all the trafficked human women wear. Its light blue stretchy material is strapped tightly across my neck, belly button, and nipples. All connected to a vertical strap covering my crotch.

"I like your skin's patterns," he says, letting his eyes drag down my body. "But I think there's something wrong with your camouflage, as beautiful as they might be."

"Those are tattoos. I don't have camouflage," I say practically to myself, knowing he doesn't understand me.

"Do you need help?" he asks, his eyes full of sincerity.

I nod aggressively.

I don't have to die today.

Do I trust the bizarrely handsome alien man in front of me? I'm not sure. He seems kind, but my trust disappeared not long after I was abducted. I don't know if it'll ever come back.

I'm not sure how long I've been dancing at this point. Everything after my abduction blurs together. The Deenz, the hive-minded purple alien fucks who captured me from Earth, give us all kinds of shots.

Downers to sleep, then uppers and aphrodisiacs to "work." It doesn't make it easy to keep track of time, and sometimes it's better to forget any of the memories you make.

"I'll try my best to help you…" He pauses. "My name is Kitaico. What's yours?"

"Leeeenuh," I tell him slowly.

"Leeeenuh," he repeats. He smiles at me, his grin full of

sharp teeth slightly more tapered than mine. I scramble backward, taken off guard by his predatory mouth.

I start to second-guess myself—that maybe this wasn't the best idea, but I'm out of options and apparently willing to gamble on a total stranger for help.

A shadow floats below my bubble as we try to figure each other out. I crane my neck down to see what it is, wondering if they'll be more beings like Kitaico.

It's not. An immense creature, about the size of a blue whale, approaches us. But there's nothing gentle looking about the giant rising quickly in the distance. While its head is whale shaped, that's where the similarities end.

The creature's sides pulse with bioluminescence as it cuts quickly through the water. Its tail is some nightmarish combo of a stingray and a scorpion. A barb at its end flashes with blue light. As it spots us, it lets out a terrifying roar and opens its mouth filled with jagged rows of fangs.

I gasp, turning back to Kitaico; his skin has changed to the deep blues of the surrounding waters. He sets his jaw and turns away from me, and for a moment, I fear he will leave me to be devoured by the creature.

As he swims, I realize his two longest head tentacles are still wrapped around my bubble, and he's dragging me toward the surface.

His powerful legs kick wildly as we climb. I can tell he's struggling to keep up his pace. Looking down, I see the monster gaining on us. It snaps its mouth, gnashing its fangs.

"Hurry, Kitaico!" I yell in vain, hoping he'll understand me.

He doesn't respond, but his camouflage shifts wildly between colors. I wonder if the effort of our escape puts his body to its limits.

I push myself against the bubble's far side as the monster's mouth closes around the bottom. With a violent crunch, it rips away a chunk of my former prison. It thrashes its head like a shark attempting to subdue its prey, but the action puts some distance between us once more.

I barely have time to hold my breath before I'm sucked out the bottom. The water crashing in makes the air rush out like a vacuum. My muscles clench painfully from the blast of water as I tumble into the warm ocean, spinning head over foot, and shut my eyes. Soon enough, I'll be nothing but fish food.

Something snakes around my ankle, tugging the skin so hard I can nearly feel it rip. Then there's something around my waist, drawing me up again.

"Leeenuh, hold on!" Kitaico yells as he hoists me into his arms, "Only a little bit closer toward the surface, the scripiat won't be able to follow much longer. He can't survive in the shallows!"

He strokes one hand behind my head and tucks my body into his chest.

I don't have enough air. My lungs burn as I involuntarily cough, and what little breath I have left escapes, bubbling upward.

Kitaico slows and his heart is still pounding against my ear.

"The scripiat returns to the depths. We are safe," he whispers.

I kick my legs weakly, pointing my finger to the surface. I can't stop myself from gulping in a deep breath of salt water and choke on its mineral taste.

"Leeenuh, we are safe now. Stay calm."

My vision blurs and I lose control of my head as it slumps onto my alien hero—it's not his fault he doesn't know I breathe air.

Darkness creeps into the edges of my vision.

I point up one more time before I lose consciousness.

We were so close.

2 /
a bitter word

I WAS sure that the female in the bubble was a hallucination. Had I finally been broken by the Great Proving? Isolation can play tricks on your mind, and I'll admit this isn't the only time I've invented someone to talk to.

The first cycle of my Proving was the easiest. I was so consumed with all the tasks and dangers required to create a new nest that I forgot my loneliness. This second and final cycle is more challenging. The daily rounds for fortifying and protecting the nest are now perfunctory. My body is on autopilot as I yearn for someone to connect with.

She can't be real.

The strange curves of her body are beautiful, even though her camouflage seems to be malfunctioning. She stands out against the blue of the deep, her brightly colored skin patterns nothing like what's around her. She also lacks any tentacles besides those that look drawn on her legs. Her head is crowned with delicate pink wisps. I wonder what they do. Could there be hidden poison barbs? The color leads me to believe so.

Maybe she's not afraid because her mate is nearby? She's relaxed as her bubble drops further and further into the depths of the sea. The women of my people, the Andjin, are constantly in hiding. Kidnapping a potential mate, while barbaric, isn't unheard of.

Males outnumber females ten to one, which is the entire reason for the time I've spent in the wilderness—to prove myself worthy of a mate.

When she speaks her soft nonsensical words, the suppression of my translator chip makes is impossible for us to understand each other. While it's true that my people prefer a simpler life than many in this universe, we do rely on tech more than most would like to admit. However, any tech to assist me is forbidden during my proving. It's considered unnecessary for my current mission—a distraction.

We must go through this trial only as the Great Mother has made us—she provides everything we need during this test.

The female's voice is sweet and melodic as she tells me her name with the strangest hit of anxiety. At first, I think it's a reaction to me, but I quickly realize she has no control over her bubble's descent.

Leeenuh needs my help.

A charge floods through my body, my camouflage shifting quickly to hide me in the open waters. The school of yellow dredlin disperses from around us. As they part, the scripiat makes itself known. It bellows, rushing for the female, its maw spread wide.

I wrap my foretentacles around Leeenuh's rugged enclosure, pushing the muscles in my legs to their limit as I drag her toward the shallows.

The beast's large body is only supported by the pressures of the deeper waters. If we can ascend quickly enough, we'll escape.

I know my camouflage is shifting wildly with my efforts, but there's no point in trying to deceive the scripiat. The female will be dead in the water if we can't outswim him.

With a sick crunching noise, I hear its jaws break into the bubble. Frantically I spin, praying to the Great Mother that I don't find her split in half.

As the bubbles clear, I see her body spinning in the currents, luckily still in one piece.

"Leeenuh, hold on!" I yell as I dive and hoist her into my arms. "We only need to get a bit higher—he can't survive in the shallows!"

She doesn't respond, but I put my hand behind her head and pump my legs furiously to ascend. I fan the webbing of my hands and toes and use their resistance against the water to move even more quickly.

I can feel the pressure shift in my body, and I know that despite the roars below us, we've evaded the danger.

"We are safe!" I whisper to Leeenuh.

She doesn't calm down. She pushes against me, sputtering and choking. Her eyes shut, and her head lolls. I pat her cheek hard, trying my best to wake her. My hand runs down her neck to support her head. Her skin is soft and smooth…and her neck is free of gills.

This female isn't aquatic.

Of course, she's not. Why would she be in an air-filled bubble under the waves if she was? I curse my stupidity and rush to break the surface of the water.

Please don't let me be too late.

The spray of the waves kisses my face with salty droplets as I make my body switch from its underwater breathing. Water rushes from my gills, running in thick rivulets down the cords of my neck.

Treading the water, the female limp in my arms, I head toward the jagged outcropping of the island. Porous, iridescent mineral formations litter the breeding gound. These pockets of space are the caves in which we build our nests.

The current provides the final push, beaching us both on the rocky shore. She's underneath me, not breathing. Her lips change from pink to blue.

I turn Leeenuh onto her side and thump my fist on her back. She's lifeless for only a second, but it feels much longer. When she finally ejects the water from her lungs, her normal breathing patterns return. Her swollen chest rises and falls as the wet fabric of her bodysuit sticks obscenely to her skin.

She coughs, and I turn her head to the side, letting the salt water work its way out of her lungs. Her body shudders, and she slumps her shoulder blades back onto the rocks.

Leeenuh's mouth opens, letting a string of raspy words fall out.

"I don't understand. I'm sorry, Leeenuh…"

She coughs again, color flooding her once-pale face.

She grips my biceps with her hands, her nails digging into my flesh, and she pulls herself to sit. I can feel her lips move next to the sensitive lobe of my ear. I wrap my arms around her torso to support her weak attempt.

"Kitaico…" she whimpers before slumping, her back arching over my arms.

Something stirs inside my chest—breathing in her scent and holding her tiny frame against my body causes something to snap into place. That small twinge multiplies quickly, turning into one all-consuming thought.

Protect.

I have to get Leeenuh back to the nearby nest. I have to keep her safe…

She's still drifting in and out when she coughs again.

I'll have to breathe for her to get her to the nest. If she is mated, touching her so intimately would be unforgivable.

I hitch her up against me, her head falling into the hollow of my neck. Joined together as one, we slide back into the sea.

I shake her roughly enough to get her attention, even though it pains me to handle her so. She has a translator chip, so I tell her my plans.

"We're going somewhere safe. It's not far, but we must swim." She stares at me, her eyes open but lids heavy. "I will breathe for you. Do you trust me?"

She cocks her head, furrowing her brows. A silence passes between us, one that feels much longer than it likely is.

She nods, setting her jaw. More strange words fall from her lips, and she wraps her legs around the small of my back. Our hips are pressing tightly against each other. For the first time since I began the Great Proving, I am self-conscious of my nakedness. Clothing, much like tech, is unnecessary during my trials. I make a conscious effort to control my mating crest. The feelers ache to explore whatever lays beneath her thin body suit. To open her sex as if she was my own kind, to mate her, to rut her, to—I stop myself, curling the tips of my tentacles back toward my hardening cock.

Miming a deep breath for Leeenuh to follow, I switch to aquatic breathing. I grimace as my gills fill again. They stretch and ache with the rush of water. The waves lick at our heads as we dip beneath its surface.

My feet press off the sharp side of the island. Leeenuh's cheeks puff outward as she holds her breath. I scan the watery expanse, looking for challengers to my…no, she's not mine. I shake my head in an attempt to clear it.

I haven't proven myself—I am undeserving.

She blows fat bubbles from her nose, and I quickly place my mouth over hers and breathe. She parts her pillowy pink lips and accepts the air I give her.

I linger over her mouth longer than I need to. My entire body tingles in anticipation of something I cannot ask Leeenuh to give me. As I pull away, I see the entrance to my nest.

The perimeter of the cave's opening is decorated with the

scales of the scripiat—the blue glinting against the iridescent purple of the island formation.

Pulling her tightly against me, I embark on the winding and narrow tunnel toward the nest's opening.

Cresting into the air pocket, Leeenuh gasps.

At first, it's for air, but as her eyes adjust, her mouth gapes at her surroundings.

Worog worms hang from the cavern's high ceiling, their purple glow illuminating the space. Their light reflects off Leeenuh's wide green eyes, the white portion of them now an angry red. Maybe her camouflage is eye based.

Only a few months are left of my proving, and my nest is nearly complete. Jewel-toned tapestries woven from dried miyhu weeds decorate the walls. They're patterns similar to the skin I was born in—a nest is not a place you should have to hide or camouflage.

I gently set her on the pool's lip, even though something inside me screams to show her more.

I want to lift the tapestry behind me and show her the dried dredlin and nuite fruit stores. Tell her I've tapped the spring from above, so fresh water will run when the cap is removed. I want her to approve of it all.

I ignore every instinct except one.

Pulling my body onto the stone floor, I lift Leeenuh and carry her to the sleeping nook. The rocks form a natural pocket, big enough for two Andjin. The bedding is fresh, as I just completed it yesterday morning. I lay her down, pulling the woven miyhu blanket over her body.

"Rest," I tell her, tucking the edge of the blanket under her chin.

For a moment, she looks like she might fight me, but I think she's too exhausted. Leeenuh sighs and wiggles her body deeper into the bedding, her scent filling the space.

As I move to the other side of the cavern, near a secondary seawater pool, she begins whispering things I can't understand.

"Sleep, Leeenuh. We can figure all of this out once you're rested."

She nods, closing her eyes. I can hear her breathing slow as she succumbs to sleep. My muscles ache from the exertion of her rescue. I pretend to inspect the pool, but instead, I run through a mental list of everything I would ask for her approval on.

Those thoughts are nothing more than folly.

We are different, she is not mine. She could even be mated to another. I am not yet even worthy of a mate.

Mate—the word feels bitter on my tongue.

"Leeenuh," I whisper as I dip my hands into the underwater garden that, just yesterday, I hoped my future mate would use as our nursery.

Leeenuh.

3 /
an accident

I RUB the tops of my feet back and forth on the soft textured blankets underneath me, stuck somewhere between incredibly rested and not wanting to leave the comfort of my bed.

Stretching my arms over my head, I flop onto my back and open my eyes.

Wait—this isn't my bed! Yesterday's misadventures flood my mind.

Kitaico sits cross-legged, his elbows propped on his knees, observing me like his own personal little museum exhibit.

"You can sleep longer if you want," he says, tilting his head as he looks at me. "Or maybe you're hungry?"

He scrambles to his feet and pulls back one of the woven curtains covering a storage nook in the wall. He produces several pieces of what looks like whole dried fish and offers me one.

I sit on the edge of the bed and take it from his hand. The fish's eyes are dangling from long stalks. I recognize them as the creatures that swam around my bubble after being dropped into this planet's ocean.

I'm momentarily sad, thinking of the glittering school of happy little fish. Everyone's gotta eat, I suppose.

I wrinkle my nose as he snaps the head and tosses it into the pool at the cave's opening. It disappears in a flash, the currents ripping it away. Knowing my luck, I'll roll my ankle and fall ass over tits into the open ocean. I make a mental note to watch my footing around the hole.

Kitaico bites a hunk off the fish and chews.

"It's good—try some," he says with his mouth full. His sharp canines ripped the flesh easily.

I copy his head-snapping technique and throw it toward the water. I miss, and it bonks off the floor and onto Kitaico's chest.

He chuckles, tossing it over his shoulder, and mimes for me to eat mine.

While I love the ocean, fish isn't really my favorite. It doesn't smell too off-putting, though. Not wanting to be rude to this strange man who saved me, I take a bite. Although I wouldn't say I love the flavor, it's not bad, either. It's salty enough to make my mouth water.

It's like fish jerky, and as I chew it, my stomach gurgles. I haven't eaten since long before the Deenz ship unceremoniously dropped my security bubble into the ocean. The dried meat is no burger and fries, but it tastes light-years better than what I've been eating.

The Deenz, the cheap bastards that they are, feed us a gray mush. The flavor and texture combination is really awful. It's like eating paste glue.

I barely realize I've scarfed down the whole fish before Kitaico snaps the head off another and hands it to me. My teeth, not as sharp as my alien friend's, struggle slightly to bite off hunks.

"Do you like it?"

I nod but turn down a third fish when he offers it. Kitaico's eyes light up with some weird sort of pride as I eat.

I'm curious if his people cook at all. The fish wouldn't be half bad rehydrated in a soup.

"Thank you, Kitaico—I'm stuffed, really." I put a hand up in refusal.

His eyes light up when I say his name, his skin rippling with red before settling down to its usual coloring of yellow with blue rings. I wonder if he has any control over his camouflaging skin, or if it feels like breathing, changing subconsciously.

"I am pleased you liked the dredlin." He puffs out his chest.

"Dredlin," I repeat. That's what these little creatures are called?

"Your accent is good. I'm surprised." Kitaico cocks his head. "Have you ever met another of my kind?"

"No," I tell him, shaking my head. I've met lots of aliens, but nothing quite like him.

"That makes sense. I don't think any Andjin has ever met one of your kind either. What is your species? Where are you from?"

"Human," I say, placing my hand to my chest. "Earth." I point upward.

"A human from Earth," he confirms. "Do you have a family on Earth?"

"No, not anymore." I think about my grandmother, who raised me, and my heart stings at the loss of her.

"I'm sorry...it is a great sadness to bear being alone." His eyes grow distant.

"Do you have a family?" I gesture to him.

"Family? Yes, I have both my parents and two brothers who live in the capital. I haven't seen them in many cycles, though—I miss them deeply. My brothers will be grown men when I next see them." A sadness creeps into his voice. I want to ask why he can't go to them, but I don't have a way to convey that with gestures alone.

"Do you have a mate?" he asks, the words rushing out.

A mate? Like a boyfriend or a husband? Even on Earth, I was chronically single.

"No."

"You're unmated and alone...that is incredibly dangerous. You are lucky to have found me and not an exiled male...who knows what would have happened to you!"

He gets flustered and doesn't seem to know what to do with his hands. They slide back over his head tentacles, and he fiddles with one in particular near his ear.

Being single on this planet seems to be a very bad thing. I gesture to him to ask if he has a mate.

"A mate? I am not yet worthy, but hopefully soon." He stands, putting his hands on his hips and surveys the cave with a broad smile, his pride akin to a midwestern dad standing on a newly built deck. "This nest is almost ready for a mate's inspection. Just a few more things to prepare."

His stance makes his crotch jut forward, and I try once again not to stare at his bizarre alien cock. Although I've gotten used to nudity, something embarrasses me at how casual he is with his nakedness.

His tentacles, on both his head and dick, are always subtly in motion. I gaze to the side to avoid staring at their gentle pulsating.

The alien must understand my shyness, and he gives me more space as if he's trying to be polite. Keeping his voice low, he asks me if I need anything.

Shifting in the bed, my full bladder pinches in my belly, and I clench my pelvic floor.

"God, I don't know if you'll be able to understand me...but is there a restroom in this place?" I say, trying to figure out the best way to convey that I need the ladies' room.

"I don't understand...maybe you can show me?"

Geez, I don't want to show him I have to pee...but I also don't want to piss myself either. I grit my teeth and take a breath.

I look him dead in his big curious eyes—then I gesture to my crotch and signal a stream of pee with my hands. I even make a whizzing noise with my mouth. It is not my finest moment.

"Pee?" I say in my weakest of voices.

"Oh, I'm so sorry, yes..." He bites his lip and turns. "Follow me."

He leads me to the far corner of the room. The floor holds a tiny tunnel full of swirling water. It's like a miniature of the opening we came in before, and I stifle the awkward laugh that is bubbling inside my chest.

The toilet is very much in the open, and while I wouldn't say I'm modest...I wouldn't say I like using the commode in front of anyone.

"You can use the relief spot whenever needed...you can do anything you'd like really in the nest until I can take you to the capital. We'll leave when it comes time for my next assessment. It's against tradition to leave my nest before that point. I would take you there sooner was this not the case...but I cannot risk being eliminated." He stares at me as if expecting a response he could understand.

"Can you turn around at least?" I wince, crossing my legs. I add a finger motion for good measure.

"Oh, my apologies," he mumbles, quickly covering his eyes and spinning away from me.

At least I don't have to get any more naked than need be with these strappy bodysuits all the bubble babes wear. I pull the crotch to the side while standing over the pool and take what feels like the longest, loudest pee of my life. The little water vortex spins the waste out quickly, and clean salt water replaces it. There's no toilet paper around, so I splash some of the cool seawater onto my crotch, which is better than nothing, I suppose.

"I'm done!" I yell over to him, and he swivels, peeking through his fingers to ensure I'm not still doing my business.

"Well, I suppose you should make yourself comfortable. I need to complete a few things around the nest."

I nod, returning to the bed, unsure of what to do with myself.

Sitting on its edge, I watch Kitaico get to work. He hauls up a line of the dredlin fish from the entrance pool—I wonder if he caught them while I slept.

His yellow fingers work swiftly, threading a cord through the gills and out of their mouths. He rips the line and ties up several in a bundle that he hangs from the ceiling—I assume to dry them and create the jerky I just inhaled. He barely pays attention to his hands, repeatedly turning back to check on me.

He has the look of my grandmother when she would make pierogi. I remember watching her hands move, seemingly on their own accord, as she gossiped with our neighbors. Her twisting and pinching of the dough was just some muscle memory forged long ago.

My travels as a bubble babe through space have proven that kindness isn't universal. I'm lucky that someone like Kitaico rescued me.

As he works, his back flexes, his muscles and lines are so close to that of a human body. It makes me wonder if maybe we share some distant ancestor. I mean, minus the head and dick tentacles. What if the eccentrics on *Ancient Aliens* aren't too off the mark?

Should I worry about what the elders of his people want to do with me? Probably. But I find myself unconcerned. If Kitaico treats me so kindly, surely his people are good.

I can't go home to Earth. The Deenz regularly told us it's off-limits. Before the Deenz decontaminate us, humans carry germs that could wipe out alien civilizations. Only the Deenz have the security clearance to "recruit" women from Earth.

Recruit and kidnap are interchangeable words, I guess.

I snap myself out of thinking about my former captors when I hear Kitaico yawn.

"Didn't sleep well?" I ask as if he can understand me. He looks at me and smiles before promptly yawning again.

Appraising the cave we're in, I come to a realization. While it's not cramped by any means…it's not some expansive place. The glow of the worms on the ceiling illuminates every corner.

There's one bed.

Of course, he didn't sleep well. I slept in the only bed, and he likely stayed up and kept watch. I'm a fucking awful guest.

He needs some sleep too. Could I convince him to take a nap? I rise from the bed and slip beside him as he works.

"You sleep now," I tell him slowly, pointing to the bed and taking the cord from his hands. "I'll do this. It doesn't look too hard." I point to the fish, which he begrudgingly hands over.

He twitches slightly and his skin ripples in waves of colors as our fingertips touch.

"You don't have to—" he starts.

"Bed. Now," I say, pointing more dramatically this time.

"Well, if you insist, I could use some rest…" He finishes his statement with another big yawn.

He sits on the edge of the bed with heavy lids and watches me work.

"You're pretty good at that, you know?" He cocks a brow. "Don't tell me I managed to save a huntress?"

I smirk and wave for him to lie back. A huntress? The thought makes me laugh. I don't know how to tell him I'm a city-loving tattoo artist. Cities and tattoos probably aren't even a thing on this planet.

He plops onto his bed with a thud, and I swear I can hear him snoring shortly after that.

After my dramatic rescue, throwing some of these weird little fish up to dry is the least I can do.

When I get about seven fish threaded on the line, I attempt to rip the cord to hang it up…but Kitaico made it look deceptively easy! No matter how hard I tug, I can't get the line to snap like he did.

He must have had some knife or blade I didn't know about.

I sneak over to the bed to see if he had set something down. I kneel beside him and check to see if he's still sleeping.

His breath is even, and his eyes are shut. I don't want to disturb the obviously tired alien, so I continue to snoop. When I stand, I catch the blue glint of something in his hand.

The silly guy must have been so tired he didn't give it to me. I kneel on the bed and reach my fingers carefully over him to his far hand. I can't make out the knife well. This half of the bed is shadowed in the darkness of the nook.

With my forefinger and thumb, I gently pinch the blade out of his hand.

The second my skin makes contact with what I assume was a knife, the hard nub opens like a petal. Before I can draw my hand back, it snaps shut over the meat of my palm, and pain courses through me.

Kitaico jerks and his hand grabs my wrist as he sits up like a bolt.

"Leeenuh, what are you doing?" He mutters, confused, before his hand tightens—his body goes ramrod straight as he flops back.

At this point, I realize it's not a blade…it's a barb and part of his body.

Stinging discomfort shoots up my arm as Kitaico writhes beside me. His face twisted in some rapture.

"Kitaico, what's happening?" I yell, trying to tug my hand free.

His longer two head tentacles wrap around me, pulling my body flat against his. The air leaves my chest with the force of the movement. We're face to face, our skin pressed up against each other, and his body is feverishly hot.

He grabs my other hand and forces our palms together. His hips grind, and I can feel his cock hardening.

No, no, no, no, no…

"Kitaico, this hurts," I say meekly, my voice almost a whisper. My past traumas force me to be as quiet and as small as I can.

His eyes shoot open when I say his name again, and he

releases me, pushing my body roughly into the far end of the bed.

The alien's body pulses in waves of black and red. The chaotic display of color deepens my fear.

He looks at his palm, the barb retracting quickly into his skin as if it was never there. His eyes raise to me, his mouth agape.

"How did you—" he looks at his other palm, gently tracing a finger down it. "There's no mark…"

I clutch my hand against my chest, the pain from his sting radiating all up my right side. There's a red starburst mark around the wound, and it throbs torturously.

"Why would you do this?" His face is splashed with hurt.

"Me? I didn't do anything!" I yelp, shaking my head, the stinging pain only deepening as the second tick by.

"You took my mating sting…but gave me nothing in return…" He looks at his palm once more. "Do you choose to reject me?"

His eyes don't leave his hand.

"I don't have a fucking stinger," I tell him, tucking my injured hand under my armpit. I hold up the other palm and try to show him.

The alien takes my hand in his, prodding the flesh at the heel of my palm, looking for a bony barb that isn't there.

"This can't be." He scowls.

"What can't be?" I ask as fat tears run down my face. I bite the inside of my cheek, trying to dull the pain now overtaking my whole body.

"Do you know what you've done?" Kitaico asks gravely.

I shake my head. He lets out a painful-sounding breath.

"I have marked you as my mate…but you cannot reciprocate. You are my mate, but I am not yours."

"I didn't know, I was looking for a knife, I wanted to help!" The pain is making me ramble. I shake my head over and over again.

"I will belong to no one now."

Kitaico is defeated as he stands. He grabs a square of woven cloth and dips it into one of the pools of water. He attempts to pass it to me, but I don't take it.

"I am sorry for your pain. It will subside soon." He pulls my hand out from under my arm and places the cool cloth onto the puncture wound. "We have much to discuss, and not long before the venom takes effect."

Shit.

no better than a pup

THIS TINY CREATURE is scared of me. She's sobbing while holding her hand tightly against her chest. Leeenuh must know nothing of my people to have inadvertently taken my mating sting.

She is my mate, but I know she doesn't honestly want me. Regardless of the lack of my mating mark—she is mine now to protect. If the sight of her in pain was unbearable to me before, her reaction to what I say next breaks my heart.

"We have much to discuss, and not long before my venom takes effect," I tell her.

Leeenuh's eyes grow wide, and I can smell her fear—her panic at what will happen next.

She babbles feverishly in a language I'll never understand, fat tears slicking down her red cheeks.

"Leeenuh, please be calm. I need you to make a decision."

Her breath stutters, and she wipes some fluid from beneath her nose with her unmarked hand.

"Good girl," I say, slowly approaching.

She allows my advances, taking deep and measured breaths, as she tries to regain control of herself. Her exhalations hit me like a warm and sweet caress.

Mine! The bond screams, wanting me to snatch her into my arms. To wrap my foretentacles around her beautifully decorated body and never let go.

But I don't—because I am not hers.

I reach for her injured hand, and she tenderly presents it. Trembling gently, I remove the cloth from her palm. My heart aches as I see the mark left by my barb.

Although the flesh is red and swollen, I can already make out the faint purple-maroon mark that my venom is etching into her warm beige skin. We're running out of time.

I take her hand and press it against my chest.

"Leeenuh, you have taken my mating sting," I tell her slowly. She sniffles as I use my other hand to brush her tangled mane from her wet cheek.

"I have marked you as my own, but I know you didn't understand what you did. I need to know what you want me to do."

Leeenuh's brows knit together, the confusion on her face a universal gesture.

"My sting, my venom, will force your body into heat. If you're anything like the females of the Andjin—and I assume you are if my barb was even present to begin with—you will cycle through three heats over the next moon's pass."

Leeenuh's mouth falls open. It closes a few times before producing noises I can't comprehend.

"I will do nothing you do not wish to do…not before the heat takes hold." I raise my hand and show her my palm. "I will not fall into the mating rut; you have not marked me as yours. If you wish to never consummate as my mate, it is your choice. I will respect any decision you make."

My voice almost cracks. I will never hurt or abuse her. I want nothing more than for my mate to want me.

Leeenuh bites her lip and stares at her hand on my chest for what feels like some eternity, not the few seconds it actually is.

My mate pulls her hand back from my chest and inspects it. She traces her delicate fingers around the mark and looks up at me.

She shakes her head.

"No?" I mumble as our eyes lock. Leeenuh waits for my reaction as if I could do anything but what she wishes of me.

"No," I affirm again. Just as something breaks deep within me, I can feel a new mission snap into place.

Protect Leeenuh, even if it's from herself.

"I promise you are safe with me," I say as I puff my chest out. The Great Mother has chosen a different path for me, and I will respect my purpose.

"Do your people go through heat?" I ask, a to-do list clicking together in my brain. My focus intensifies on being exactly who Leeenuh needs me to be.

I grimace as she shakes her head no.

"It will be overwhelming. You'll stop at nothing to find a cock to mount." My mate gulps. "But I will ensure you are kept safe and unmated, as are your wishes."

Leeenuh lurches toward me, her arms wrapping tightly around my neck. When she buries her face into me, I can feel her tears roll down my neck, welling up by my collarbone.

She is mine, and…that's all that matters. I draw her scent into my lungs. I have no idea what the future holds, but even if this is as close as she'll let me get—I'll happily take it.

Putting some space between us, I cradle her chin in my hand. I stroke a tear away with the pad of my thumb, trying to convey the glowing adoration I feel inside.

"Ankh Chew," she speaks between sniffles before notching herself against me once again.

I should push her away once more. I should ready myself for the onslaught of my mate's heat.

Maybe I'm not as strong as I think I am…perhaps I won't be able to resist her. Even if she wishes not to have me now, I know the frenzy she'll be in soon will convince her otherwise.

I promise to protect this version of my mate, no matter what.

Something warm and wet swipes up my neck, and when it hits the lobe of my ear, I can feel my cock harden. My skin knows what's happening before I do, and it shifts to an amorous purple.

The feelers of my mating crest that circle my shaft search for her skin to grasp.

I moan as my mate takes my ear into her mouth. She digs her nails into my back, pulling me closer. I push her roughly, and she falls onto the bed with a dull thud. Leeenuh inhales sharply, as if the wind has been knocked from her.

She raises a hand over her head. The small tuft of brown fur in her armpit releases a concentration of her scent into the nest.

My engorged cock is painfully hard when my foretentacles instinctively shoot out to grab Leeenuh. They slide down her body, ripping the coverings at the crotch, before the limbs wrap around her ankles. With a tug, they pull her knees apart. As they fall open, the scent of her cunt hits me like a crashing ocean wave. She pushes the torn damp blue strip of fabric resting over her crotch to the side with one finger.

Leeenuh has glistening folds almost the same color as the mating mark. I can see the pulse throbbing near her cunt's apex.

Bringing her other hand to her beautiful sex, she runs a finger up her slit. She points it to me and slides the wet digit between my lips, brushing over my sensitive fangs. A sparking feeling flutters down my spine. She is all sweetness, and she is mine.

I lean over her, our faces nearly touching. My crest's feelers push and pull through her wetness. They pulsate—grabbing for any bit of flesh they can hold. As they stroke my mate's cunt, she arches against me. All while I suck her sweetness from her finger.

Her taste is intoxicating, and only when she moans, "Kitaico," do I snap back to reality. I jerk up, my crest's limbs flailing at the loss of her.

"Leeenuh, no!" I yell as I push away from her with my hands. Unfortunately, my foretentacles refuse to release their grip on her ankles; their urge to rut our beautiful mate is too strong.

"Puhweez uck mi Kitaico!" she mewls, and throws her head back, writhing in my hold.

As I push our bodies apart, I try to think of anything but my mate, hoping my tentacles will release the grip on her legs. When my mind can only conjure up her—I change tactics.

Protect her. Protect her. Protect her… I repeat to myself over and over again.

"You don't want this. It's just the venom…this will be over soon, sweet Leeenuh!" I try to comfort her, all while attempting to get my limbs back under my control.

"Uch mi!" she cries, wiggling her hand down between her legs, rubbing frantic circles toward the top of her cunt. "Uch mi Kitaico, ease!"

I wish I could understand her, but I keep up my tension, not wanting to break my promise. She makes needy noises in my grip while her hand slides back and forth over her pretty little cunt.

"Ust et mi coom, lease jus mak mi coom, Kitaico!" She bites her lip and arches her hips. Her every muscle is taut.

"Leeenuh," I whisper in some frustrated exasperation. She unravels as soon as her name falls from my lips—as if saying her name is all that she needed to climax.

Her legs jerk straight, she moans, her head falling to the side. Her breathing slows, and Leeenuh hums little harmonic moans as she basks in the afterglow of her orgasm.

My longer foretentacles release their grip on her ankles slowly, one dragging down between my spent mate's breasts. It briefly slides down her slit, triggering another moan from my sleepy Leeenuh. As if jealous, my crest's many appendages pulse.

I snatch back the betraying foretentacles and hold them under my arms, afraid they'll not be satisfied for long. I lift the slack Leeenuh, position her more comfortably in the bed, and tuck her beneath the blankets, kissing her forehead but wanting to do so much more.

My cock throbs, being this close to her. I can feel my foretentacles wiggling their way out from under my clamped biceps. My cock's head leaks a drop of precum as I spring back, my legs taking my body as far into the opposite corner as possible. Far enough away that my tentacles won't be able to grip her. They grasp futilely behind me in her direction.

Leeenuh rustles around in the sheets, and I pray she stays sated for just a little while longer. I beg the Mother to let her be truly asleep. Meanwhile, I pace my breathing to control the thudding of my hearts. With frustration, I stare down at my erection and curse my lack of control. I shouldn't have touched her.

Turning away from my hopefully sleeping mate, I rest my forearm and head against the rocky wall of the nest. I lean over the relief hole and fist my painful length.

The touch of my fingertips is too much, the friction of sliding skin making me wince.

I think of Leeenuh, of her dripping cunt. How she moaned my name and must have been begging for my touch.

Picturing the beautiful agony on her face, I can feel the whole of my crest coil and tighten, begging me for release.

"Leeenuh," I moan, snapping my eyes shut. As if on cue, the long foretentacle that dipped through my mate's sex slips between my lips. The taste of her fills my mouth.

My ass clenches and seed pulses from my cock like a geyser, its every throb pushing me further into ecstasy.

When I open my eyes, the semen drips from my fist clenched over the head of my cock. It's a poor substitute for the clenched heat of what I think Leeenuh's cunt will be.

The pale purple liquid is sucked out in the vortex of spinning water.

I am no better than a pup.

I have to learn to control myself. I cannot hurt Leeenuh!

My foretentacles slack post-release, relaxing against my back. I grab a lashing of cord and roughly bind the two tentacles from my head against the sides of my body. The woven dried seaweed bites almost painfully into my skin. I tie another knot.

I will not hurt her.

5 /

just a little guy

PRESSING MY THIGHS TOGETHER, I realize my crotch is tight and feels rug burnt. I'm wrapped tightly in the woven blanket from Kitaico's bed. Pushing myself up to my elbows, I try to clear the sleep from my eyes, blinking rapidly, but I'm so confused.

What in the fuck happened last night?

I run my hand through my hair, and flinch. Bringing my palm close to my face, I find a swollen and tender red mark on my skin.

Kitaico…stung me? As I trace delicately around the swirling mark, bits and pieces of last night become clearer. Me reaching for what I thought was a knife, the pain of his sting, and the shocked look of the alien who rescued me.

I remember only a little of what he said, something about a heat and mates? That was all before things got crazy…

Oh god, I tried to jump Kitaico's bones!

My pussy hurts because I gave myself a friction burn after getting myself off when Kitaico pushed me away. How he held me down with his two longer tentacles and grimaced as I scratched the old record.

I'm almost embarrassed to look up when I hear a rustling from the other side of the cave. But I know there's no hiding in his small underwater home. I'm going to have to face him.

I raise my eyes trepidatiously. Kitaico stands about five feet away from his bed. In one hand he holds a shell and in the other he has a large flat seaweed leaf full of slices of something blue and glistening.

When I look at his face, the rest of the night falls into place. He said the word "mate."

"Good morning, Leeenuh!" He smiles broadly, his fangs crest over the top of his full lower lip ever so slightly. But past the bright first impression, I realize something is off.

Kitaico's eyes wear deep eggplant-colored bags. His two longest tentacles coming from his head are lashed tightly against his torso. And strangest of all, my nudist companion is wearing a skirt over his giant alien dick.

My gaze lingers a bit too long on his covered crotch before Kitaico clears his throat. His smile falters as I look up at him.

"We should probably talk," I say, wrapping my arms around myself. I try to focus on the strange bindings he's made himself. The yellow alien's color shifts to match the swirling blue of the waters near the entrance to the cave.

"Oh, these?" He poses. "These are to keep the brothers behaving. They were very..." Kitaico struggles to find the word, closing his eyes as he thinks. "They were very inconsiderate of our situation last night." His eyes shoot open triumphantly as if he's won some prize for knowing exactly what to say.

"They were inconsiderate? You can't control them?" I ask.

I know he can't understand me, but it's so strange to have to play charades when someone is speaking your language. I tap on my chin, scrunching up my face in thought before pointing to my arm and raising up.

"Think to move?" he asks, tilting his head. He's still for a moment as I watch the gears in his head turn.

"Think about moving my foretentacles?" He nods his chin down toward the tightly tied rope around his chest, and his brows knit. "No, my foretentacles think for themselves. Which is one reason I want to apologize for last night. If I did anything you didn't want me to do while unencumbered by my venom, I would ask for your deepest forgiveness."

So, some of his limbs literally have a mind of their own? That's interesting.

"It's okay, Kitaico. Can we just talk about what happened? Everything's kind of fuzzy." I do my best to mime as I talk.

"Your memory is hazy, yes?" He frowns and I nod.

He comes to the bed and sits near me. He hands me the shell, filled with what I assume is freshwater, and sets the leaf of food between us.

"Drink first, you must be thirsty," he says, and I do. He's right, I'm parched. The water cools my dry throat and I down the rest quickly. "Especially after all the moisture you lost last night."

I raise my brows, confused at his meaning as I drink.

"Your *cunt* was incredibly slick, Leeenuh," he says matter-of-factly.

I spray water from my lips, sputtering the water everywhere, unable to process the words he's just said in any other way.

"Did you choke?" Kitaico's skin rolls a deep gray color as his face switches to one of worry.

Did I choke on my water when the alien mentioned how wet my cunt was?

Yah, ya fucking betcha'.

"Sorry, yeah no, I'm okay!" I hold my hand up as a sign that I'm fine.

His face is one of disbelief, but he continues. "I would be incredibly grateful for your forgiveness, though."

Kitaico stares at his lap as if he's awaiting my answer.

"Of course, there's nothing to forgive...I think maybe if you just explain things to me again." I put my hand on his and smile, hoping I can convey that I'm not angry with him. "Tell me what's happening."

Pointing at the swirled red mark on my other palm. Kitaico looks at my face, then my palm, and plasters a smirk on his lips.

"You're my mate," he whispers.

"Me?" I question, pointing to my chest somewhat incredulously.

"Yes, you, Leeenuh. The Great Mother has given me a beautiful mate before I have even finished the Great Proving. Although she works in ways I do not understand yet, I will be thankful." Kitaico holds his own hand up. He points to a bump under the skin near his wrist. "I know we are not the same species, but we must be similar enough. My mating barb should only appear when a suitable breeding female is near. Even though you can't mark me as your own, I will uphold my end of this mate bond." Kitaico grabs my hand and clasps it over his chest.

"I don't know if I'm ready to be someone's mate..." I mutter as if he can understand me. He might not translate my words, but he must get my sentiment.

"I would never force you to do anything that you do not wish to," he says before placing my hand back into my own lap. His face is so earnest I have no choice but to take him at his word.

Kitaico could have had his way with me last night, and I would have been more than willing.

"So Leeenuh, what is it you want?" he whispers.

I've heard about mates before—they're fairly common in most alien cultures. I've always assumed it's more of a biological response than love. Like the feeling that spurs salmon to spawn. I know it's kind of like a marriage, though, and while I'm sure Kitaico is very nice, I don't think a thirty something tattoo artist from Minneapolis is the girl for him.

My seasonal depression alone can't handle the Minnesota winters. How the fuck am I going to handle living in a cave?

I wish there was some way to convey without words that I think he's a lovely alien, and that I'm so glad that he saved me from what I'm sure would have been a watery grave...but I don't know if I'm ready to procreate with a handsome man I just met.

But there's not. So I ever so ineloquently point to my crotch under the rough blanket and shake my head no.

For the briefest of seconds, I can see the hurt flash behind his eyes. But he morphs it quickly into a broad grin, the one where his fangs are on full display.

"Understood. I shall control myself, and these ruffians"—he nods down to his bound appendages—"during your heats. I hope you will allow me to make you comfortable in between. Even if we are not destined to mate, the Great Mother would want me to ensure your comfort, to protect you. Can we agree on that?" His voice is so damn hopeful that it breaks my heart a little.

When I nod in agreement, he smiles and brings the tray of food up to eye level. He grabs a slice of blue meat between his fingers and holds it up to my mouth.

"Oh, I can do it myself. It's alright," I tell him politely, reaching for a fresh slice.

I jolt when he bats my hand away.

"It's customary that I feed my mate after her first heat. It is very important in my culture to provide for your partner." He puffs his chest out.

Since I'm not having sex with this poor guy, I guess I can at least let him feed me. I part my lips and wait.

Kitaico places one of the blue slices into my mouth, his fingers lingering a bit too long on my lower lip to be some accidental touch. When he pulls his hand away, he stares at me, waiting for my reaction.

I chew, a bit hesitantly at first. But hot damn, does it taste good, even though it's raw. Sushi really wasn't my thing, again with the whole not liking fish, but it's way better than I expected. I don't even have to try to find a polite way to choke it down.

"This is fantastic," I say as I swallow. Whatever it is tastes like citrus and spice.

And before I can get another word, Kitaico is already shoving another piece into my mouth.

"It's skalpin! An apex predator and quite the delicacy. When I checked the security of the nest this morning, I found this little guy peeking around the entrance. He barely knew I was there before I dispatched him."

As my translator chip shows me images of the skalpin, it is the exact opposite of a little guy. The huge dark blue scaled snake almost looks like a water dragon. Its open maw is full of lethal looking teeth and its reptilian eyes dart menacingly as it weaves in and out of the seaweed. It's gotta be at least as big as Kitaico.

But it's also fucking delicious.

I let him feed me a few more bites, and all the while, he stares at me like a kid at his new puppy. I mean, I don't want him to breed with me, but I could get used to being waited on hand and foot. Finally, when I'm full, I put my hand up to stop him.

"It's so good, but no more!" I tell him, and he smirks, dropping the fish back onto the seaweed.

"It pleases me to see your hunger sated, Leeenuh. Do you mind if I finish the rest?"

I gesture for him to help himself. Kitaico holds the leaf like a funnel against his lips, dropping the remaining hunks of sea dragon into his mouth. His cheeks are full, and he looks at me longingly as he chews.

But just at that moment, other pressing needs arise.

"Um, Kitaico, can I use the facilities?" I point over to the corner where the toilet is.

Kitaico's color changes, and he stands quickly.

"Of course, I'm sorry, I didn't think—go ahead!" He stumbles over his words and backs up enough to let me by.

I push the blanket back, fully intending on making my way over to the weird little water toilet. But when the blanket is gone, the cold air hits my bare pussy. My bodysuit is completely torn from my crotch. I cover it with my hands and look back up at Kitaico. My cheeks are burning with embarrassment.

"Oh, yes, the brothers tore that, didn't they?" As if summoned by their name, they wriggle under their restraints. Kitaico ignores them, and in one swift motion, pulls the woven wrap skirt off his hips and hands it to me.

I grab it quickly, tying it around my waist and thanking him before I realize he's nude again. Despite the pubic tentacles' futile attempts to find purchase, his hard cock remained unyielding.

I stand, making my way to the potty as quickly as I can. Kitaico keeps his back to me, so at least I don't have to stare at his bizarre dick tentacles. But as I do my business, I can't help but think about how good they felt, like a hundred fingers working my pussy at once.

How strong is that venom of his, and how the fuck long until I cycle into heat? These seem like important questions to ask.

I finish and run my hands through the water that streams off the cave wall nearby. I splash some of the cool liquid onto my sore vag. Last night was a blur, but could I have really been that horned up to rub one out this aggressively?

I adjust his woven skirt and walk back over, clearing my throat to let him know I've finished.

When he turns around, I hold my palm up, pointing to what I now know is his species mating mark.

"Kitaico, explain more?" I ask, shrugging my shoulders like I don't understand. I need more details. When will my next heat hit?

Can we do anything to make sure I don't masturbate any more of my skin away?

6 /
strung up

"KITAICO, ECKSPLHAN MOAR." Leeenuh says in her strange tongue. But her intent is clear as she points at the mating mark now permanently etched on her skin.

I dig my fang into the meat of my cheek, hurt for a moment. But Leeenuh isn't from this world, and she's not of the Andjin—how can I ever expect her to know anything about my world? I force a smile, hoping it brings her comfort.

Last night, I made up my mind not to reveal to her that Andjin mate for life. I'll be devastated if Leeenuh doesn't choose to stay with me, but I recognize that it's my burden alone to shoulder. If we can get through her heats unscathed, and I get her to the capital to have my translator chip turned back on—maybe then we can find common ground.

We just need to get through these heats. As hard as it will be for the both of us, I know we can do it together.

"You accepted the sting of my mating barb. In my culture, when a couple wishes to join together, we exchange venom, which activates the mating bond. Through no fault of your own, you are now my mate," I tell her as calmly as I can.

Leeenuh frowns, but waves her hand, signaling for me to continue. With each step closer, my heart races and I extend my hand to grasp hers. I turn her palm over and gently trace the intricate purple swirling mark, feeling the raised texture beneath my fingertips. It's beautiful on her strange skin.

"My venom will force you to cycle through two more heats before the Korlyan moon completes its pass around Sontafrul 6. I wish I could take you to the capital, but it's not safe. There are far too many exiled males in the nesting grounds during the Great Proving. If they sense a female in heat, they'll do anything to steal you." Leeenuh's eyes go wide. "Do not worry, I won't allow them to get their filthy tentacles on you!" I puff out my chest with pride.

"Once your heats pass, it will be much safer to travel, and I will do everything I can to make sure you're comfortable until then. As I promised before, I won't touch you if you don't wish it. I can even leave the next time if you think that would be help-ful. Would you like me to leave when your next heat arrives? Would you feel safer? I would stand guard just right outside."

Leeenuh shakes her head quickly from side to side.

"No. down't leeavuh mi awone Kitaico, I down't wahnt twu hurk meyeself," she blurts.

I clasp my hands over her much smaller one. If I can't rut her, I can at least protect her.

"I won't leave you, but is there anything I can do to make you more comfortable?"

Her fingers brush against the taut lashing that secures my foretentacles to my torso, causing a slight twinge of discomfort. She points to her own wrists, gesturing as if she wants me to bind her.

"You want me to tie you up?" I ask, scratching my head. "Why would I do that?"

I would understand if maybe she wished for me to restrain

myself… but why would I ever consider tying her up? I have to quickly push the image of Leeenuh being strung up in my bed out of my mind. The thought brings great joy to the brothers flanking me, while a pleasant warmth radiates from my groin.

Leeenuh's face contorts into an embarrassed expression, her lips drawing tightly together. She clenches her fist tightly and vigorously rubs her other hand against it. With a wince, she gestures toward her cunt.

"Oh…ohhh." I swallow, my tongue feels thick.

In her pursuit of pleasure, Leeenuh fell victim to my venom and suffered an injury. The weight of guilt settles in my stomach as I realize this is entirely my fault. Despite not meaning to, I am burdened with a feeling of shame.

"Are you okay?" I ask softly.

"Just sorah." She nods unconvincingly.

"Leeenuh, let me help," I plead with her, already standing and making my way to my stores. She talks in her soft gibberish language as I do. From her tone, I'm sure she's turning down my offer of help, but I won't allow her to suffer any more than I've already allowed her to. I grab the shell filled with salve from the spot just above the dried dredlin.

Leeenuh looks nervous when I spin around. I return to her side, placing the shell in her hands.

"This salve is good for burns, both from friction and heat. You must work it liberally into the affected area," I instruct her. She takes the shell and sniffs, wrinkling her nose at the medicinal scent. "It will help."

"Ank chew, Kitaico," she says, dipping two fingers into the thick balm. She pulls the blanket up over her lap before sliding her hand underneath.

Spinning around quickly to give her privacy, my breath catches in my throat. Leeenuh is touching her cunt, and I have to pretend as if I'm unaffected.

It's not sexual, Kitaico! Get it together, you're no better than a pup. Your mate is hurt and here you are thinking with your cock. Do better.

But as I yell at myself inside my head, I distract myself with a plan for Leeenuh.

Once the nesting period for the Great Proving is over, I can take Leeenuh to the capital. I hope her third heat is over by then, as it'll be much safer to travel. I wish I could take her there sooner, but I can't risk forfeiting my rights to mate—especially if Leeenuh is who the Great Mother intended for me.

What happens once we get to the capital, I'm not sure. I've never heard of a situation like the one I've found myself in now, but maybe the elders have some wisdom I don't.

"Um dunn." Leeenuh's soft voice cuts through my inner monologue.

When I glance behind, she offers me the shell, uncertain of where to wipe her sticky fingers. I quickly grab the container, and instead of grabbing her a cloth, I use my hand to clear the excess balm off her fingers. Leeenuh's mouth drops open in shock as I do.

"Let me know if you need more," I tell her quickly before putting the salve back into the stores.

As I carefully place the shell back onto the shelves, I slyly take a moment to smell the leftovers in my hand. Despite medicinal herbs and the fat that suspends them, I can still detect her intimate scent.

The delicious scent of her hits my nervous system like an explosion, and I inhale deeper. Blood rushes to places it shouldn't, and I'm left searching for another wrap to cover my rapidly hardening cock. I tie it on quickly but am less than pleased at the tenting of my wrap. I suppose it's better than brandishing uncovered. Leeenuh seems uncomfortable with my nakedness.

I grab the driftwood stool I fashioned together at the beginning of my Great Proving and face the bed. I try to cross my leg casually over the other one in an attempt to hide my willful erection.

I am sure I look incredibly awkward.

"Today, I will work on something to restrain your hands, Leeenuh. I do not wish you to inflict any more pain on your cunt."

Leeenuh nods, her cheeks staining a red color. The color is pleasing to me for some reason, even if her poor skin's camouflage seems nearly broken.

"Kan eye elp?"

I cock my head, not understanding her. She points to the knots around my bound foretentacles. Does she want to help with making the restraints?

"No, no, let your mate handle such things. Rest for now, Leeenuh. Kitaico can take care of you!" I flash her a broad grin.

"Em nought tyurd!" She seems annoyed by my suggestion.

I thought females loved naps and being taken care of? Maybe the human females are different than Andjins ones in that regard?

"Sleep for a bit. We've got nothing but time to wait until your heats are over. Why not nap?"

She sighs, as if in resignation, and flops her head back into the nest. Even if I'm as frustrated as Leeenuh, I can't let it prevent me from being an excellent mate.

So, the task at hand is restraints for when sweet little Leeenuh becomes the wild, cock-crazed female of last night.

I will have no problem making the ropes, but I worry with all her struggling that they'll dig into her wrists and injure her still. Maybe something soft can be used as a buffer?

I stand, scratching my head.

I could harvest some torun sponges to pad out the wrist portion—I know there's a wild patch right near the entrance of the nest.

I sneak a quick glance at Leeenuh out of the corner of my eye, trying not to draw attention. She pulls the thick blanket up higher under her chin and closes her eyes.

I knew she needed rest. Maybe the Great Mother was right about picking me as her mate.

I wait until her breathing slows and I'm sure she's sleeping before I slip out the nest entrance and into the cool salt water.

50

7 /
playing doctor

THE CONSTANT BUZZ *of my tattoo machine becomes a soothing white noise, heightening my concentration. Every stroke matters, especially the delicate purple lines, as a single mistake could jeopardize the line-work of my current design.*

"You know that's forever, right?" my grandmother says.

But Grandma has been dead for years.

When I turn my head, there's no sturdy woman glaring disapprovingly at me. Oddly enough, the smell of her hairspray lingers in the air. Her hairstyle remained unchanged, with its smooth and lacquered appearance, since before I was born. She always smelled faintly of Aqua Net.

As I gaze back at my work, I notice the swirling purple mark gradually forming into a distinct shape. With my palm as the canvas, the jab of the needles in my machine is more than a dull ache. I use a clean cloth to carefully wipe away the excess ink from my skin.

A tingling sensation courses through the vortex etched on my hand, as if it's awakening. The marks on my body ignite, sending waves of searing heat through my flesh. With the flickering flames of the tiny campfire cradled in my palm, I press it against my chest, feeling its pulsing heat—I want its warmth despite the pain.

I shoot up in the bed, my breath coming in quick gasps—*it was only a dream.*

I stare at my tattoo, the mating sting that Kitaico marked me with. For the first few weeks after my abduction, I used to dream of Grandma every night, the only enduring link to Earth my mind could summon. It was always her tight embraces that made me feel safe, or the aroma of a hot tater tot hot dish, as she poured me a glass of wine in her cozy apartment kitchen.

You know that's forever, right?

Just like a tattoo, I have a feeling this mark will be difficult to remove. But forever? Maybe Kitaico could tell me how to do it… but would he be upset that I want to know if the mark will disappear? Would I even be able to get my point across?

I scan the cave, looking for my yellow protector, but he's nowhere to be found.

I seriously doubt there are any hidden spaces I don't know about in here, but that doesn't stop me from crawling out of the bed and pulling back the curtain to his storage space.

As I pull back the fabric, I'm greeted with the slightly pungent odor of stores of dried fish, woven mats, a strange purple fruit, and various primitive tools. The space is packed full, and there's no sign of Kitaico or any secret spaces.

So, the big yellow softie really left me here, even with all his claims of being my protector against the dangers of his world.

My heart thumps in my chest. Even though there's no imminent threat, it doesn't mean my brain doesn't instantly start catastrophizing.

But outside that nearby entry, just beyond its swirling blue waters, lies some scary shit.

Giant scorpion-whale-shark thing? Check. Horned-up exiled

aliens that want nothing more than me in heat? Double check. Currents that I doubt I can maneuver well enough to get to the surface? Triple check.

I don't know what to do, so I sit on the edge of the bed and pull my knees against my chest. How have I become so utterly reliant on a near stranger? Sweat begins to collect at the back of my legs.

The water at the entrance ripples, and I brace myself for what is surely a terrifying sex-crazed alien exile to burst through the pool.

But instead, it's just Kitaico. He pulls himself up onto the cave ledge using his elbows—his arms full of soft-looking purple puffs. Despite the lack of use of his arms, Kitaico stumbles only slightly as he rises to his feet. The impressive muscles of his core engage as he stands to his full height, towering above me. I let my eyes trail his body as the rivulets of water stream down into the defined vee of his hips.

My arms swing wide around his body, and his yellow skin shifts to a deep blue. I'd like to think I'm only hugging him because I'm relieved, but as my fingers slide down his lats muscles, I know it's just an excuse to touch him.

"Leeenuh, are you alright?" he asks as he drops the spongy things in his arms. He clasps my chin in his hand and tilts my head up to meet his gaze.

"I'm okay, really." I relax my jaw and lean back, realizing that I've let my anxiety get the better of me. "Where were you?"

"I didn't think you'd wake up before I returned. I was just collecting torun right outside the door. I would never leave you unprotected—never."

Kitaico sets his jaw, letting his hands fall from my face to my sides as he pulls me closer.

The warmth coming from his slick skin is surprising, and I can't help but cuddle myself into him.

I'm lost in the sensation of skin on skin. The second his

restrained tentacles begin to wiggle at my sides, I'm snapped from the momentary daze.

I step back, much to Kitaico's disappointment. The loss of his body heat is jarring.

I shouldn't give him the wrong idea though, right?

Hell, I don't want to give my own body any ideas, despite how nice he feels.

And that's probably for the best because my jump off the bed has agitated my already angry vag. My thighs chafe against the raw skin between my legs when I walk.

"You're still injured. Don't move," he says.

Before I can parse what's happening, he's carefully lifting me off the ground and cradling me in his arms.

"I'm perfectly fine to walk—put me down, Kitaico!" I yelp, batting at his chest.

Only when we return to the bed does he gently lay me on my back.

"Stay there," he says, going back to his curtain-covered stores.

He returns with the shell of salve from earlier, and I reach for the medicine.

But Kitaico pulls it back.

"If you'll allow me, I'd like to ensure you aren't getting an infection. I don't know if you're more susceptible to the environment here than I am."

I raise my brows, realizing that he's asking me to put my rug-burnt pussy on display.

"Kitaico, really, it's not that bad—"

"I would never forgive myself if something happened to you." He frowns.

Despite my all-consuming embarrassment at the idea of him slathering my pussy in medicine, I also know that he's probably right. I really have no idea how my human body will react to this new environment.

"Fine," I tell him. I part my legs and give him the access he wants.

I stare at him as his camouflage ripples and his breath catches slightly in his throat.

"Leeenuh, this must be incredibly painful…I'm so sorry," he mutters.

"It's probably not as bad as it looks."

"Will you allow me to apply the salve? I fear you might miss something if you do it yourself again. The coverage doesn't seem very even. The skin where it was applied properly seems to fare much better than the rest."

He wants to touch my pussy.

"You want to touch me…here?" I ask him, my cheeks ablaze as I point to my crotch.

"Just to apply the medicine thoroughly, I promise to be respectful, as your mate should be," he says seriously, rolling his shoulders back.

Sure, he's seen it already—and to be honest, he's probably right about the whole infection deal.

"Fine," I mutter in defeat.

A major thing that the Deenz, my abductors, taught me is not to expect kindness. I'm lucky that I've ended up here with Kitaico. He's light-years better than my former captors. I shouldn't complain, some girls had it way worse. I didn't even have to participate in some of the seedier activities—mostly just bubble dancing and serving drinks for the high-paying aliens.

Is it weird that I feel lucky to be here?

It always shocked me to see how many of us human gals were abducted by the Deenz…did anyone know the truth about where we ended up?

Are any of us on an episode of Unsolved Mysteries *yet?*

I focus on the ceiling as I wait for Kitaico to do what needs to be done. Another trick I've picked up since being a bubble babe? An unhealthy ability to disassociate.

But try as I might, I can't ignore his hands. Slowly and intentionally, his fingers make contact with the smooth skin where my thigh and pussy connect.

My breathes hitches, and his fingers twitch over my lips.

His fingertips are slick with the salve as he prods closer to my center. The pain of my irritated skin slips to the back of my mind as he ignites the pleasurable nerves of my sex.

"The skin you covered properly is already looking so much better. I will be thorough in my application to your cunt, Leeenuh," He slides his fingers between my inner and outer labia, and my hips buck slightly.

For Chrissakes, he's just trying to take care of me and I'm thrusting into his fucking hands. Maybe with the lubricating salve, he won't notice the growing wetness.

His fingers stop just below my clit.

"You are built so differently than our kind, but your cunt is still beautiful to behold. Like a delicate shell that holds a precious pearl," he whispers.

The air between us feels charged with electricity. Maybe it's just his venom still coursing through my veins. There's a part of me that wants him to take advantage of the situation, despite my tender flesh.

"You know, maybe it might be smart for you to help me out next heat, just so I don't hurt myself." I say aloud, knowing that he'll not be able to understand me.

It's only when he looks up at me that I realize that I've been staring at him.

I look away, feeling my cheeks burn hotter than before.

It's gotta be the venom.

"I don't understand, Leeenuh," he says, finishing his application in a gentlemanly manner, unfortunately. As he pulls his hand away from my crotch, his fingers linger and delicately trace the intricate lines of my tentacle tattoo wrapping around my thigh.

When it comes to tattoos, I have a strong affinity for all things nautical. The ocean, to me, has always carried an aura of pure magic, perhaps because of my landlocked upbringing in Minnesota.

"At first I thought these were some strange broken camouflage, but your skin decorations are beautiful."

"Oh, I take it you guys don't have tattoos." I try my best to ignore the feeling of his fingers as they linger on my skin. Speaking, I notice Kitaico tilting his head, trying to understand my words.

How do I even convey the idea of tattoos to an alien without a shared language?

"Tattoo," I repeat slowly, tapping the oceans scene on the underside of my bicep—a spot less dangerous than my inner thigh.

"Tahtooo." Kitaico overenunciates the word like he does my name.

"Good." I smile, tracing over the curve of the wave on my arm.

"You drew those on yourself?" he asks, his eyebrows shooting up as the realization kicks in.

"Well, I didn't draw this one—but I could." It'd be an awkward angle to attempt on my own. But there's no point in confusing him, so I just nod.

"The Andjin don't have these tahtooos. I fear they would ruin our cloaking…but on you, they're perfect."

An extraterrestrial saying something nice is a pleasant surprise, especially when compared to the rude comments I've received while bubble dancing.

"Maybe you could draw something beautiful for the nest? Something to help pass the time." He pauses, his jaw setting, and he stands before he continues. "Before your next heat."

Oh, the damper on everything, the fucking heats.

"Speaking of, I was out to get those." He points to the pile of purple puffs he dropped earlier. "To pad out the restraints. Something that's supposed to keep you from hurting yourself shouldn't be uncomfortable."

When he stands again, I see that his sentient head tentacles must have been squirming the entire time he was touching me. The skin, normally yellow, is now inflamed with a bluish hue where it was constricted against his torso.

I flip the wrap skirt down, tucking my ripped bubble babe bodysuit gingerly into the waistband.

I can't bear to see Kitaico suffer when he's putting in so much effort into taking care of me. I slip out of the bed with caution, determined to hide any signs of pain from him.

He watches me as I cross the room over to the purple pile of what I now think might be alien sea sponges. I reach for one, and then hold it out to him.

"You first," I point to the tentacles that he calls the unruly brothers.

"I'm fine," he waves me off.

Fine my ass.

I can see now, on closer inspection, that the lashings are cutting so tightly into him that his blue blood is welling up where it's tied the tightest.

"No."

I reach out for one of the ties, but his hand quickly grabs mine.

"I can't control them. They'll touch you." His face is deadly serious and his eyes narrow.

But I can't let him keep hurting himself.

"We'll figure something out," I say before ripping the knot free.

It takes all of ten seconds before the brothers ratchet around me and pull me tightly against him. Kitaico's skin flashes purple, and I look up just as his eyes darken.

8 /
good boys

THE DAMP AIR in the cave suddenly feels heavy and suffocating, making it difficult to take a deep breath. Without warning, my foretentacles wrap quickly around Leeenuh, bringing her plush body tightly against my own.

Panic surges through me as I see the brothers explore Leeenuh's breasts. Their forceful kneading on her skin continues, and I am left feeling utterly helpless in stopping them. As our torsos touch, her body's warmth radiates through my skin.

Meeting her eyes, I am overcome with the need to apologize, unable to find the right words.

"I'm so sorry Leeenuh, I'm sorry. I told you I can't control them—"

Without warning, she leans forward, and I can feel the softness of her lips against mine. The sudden, unexpected gesture leaves me motionless, my muscles frozen in surprise.

As her tongue delicately explores the depths of my mouth, the shock intensifies. I feel the sharpness of my fangs being tested, a surprising sensation that has me leaning closer to her. The meeting of our mouths overwhelms me as I surrender to this unexpected connection.

As I let her explore, the sound of our hearts pounding in my ears drowns out everything else. Strange as it is, this new sensation fills me with a rush of exhilaration. I let my eyes close in silent contentment.

I don't even realize that the brothers have loosened their grip until she finally breaks our contact. As if she was in some haze, she shakes her head quickly. A tendril from her pink mane falls onto her forehead.

"Eyem sowwee, eye dount noh wat kam ovuh mi," she says in a daze.

"I, I'm sorry," is the only thing I can manage to get out, still in shock myself.

She gently places her hands on each of the brothers and strokes them softly.

"Issa okay, cahm downa."

She speaks with a gentle tone, her voice like a melody that caresses my ears. Her touch is a sensation from another world, sending shivers down my spine. In her presence, my senses awaken, and an undeniable surge of desire rushes through me as my cock hardens.

I can see she's aware of it, but it's almost as if she chooses to overlook my body's undeniable reaction. The sound of my breathing intensifies as I try to contain my growing desire. Despite the stiffness that engulfs me, she seems determined to disregard it, leaving me longing for her touch.

Only when my placated foretentacles release Leeenuh completely do I feel her step back. Losing her body warmth sends a shiver down my spine, leaving me cold and disconnected.

"I'm sorry, again, so sorry," I say as I turn to grab a woven cloth to tie around my waist in an attempt to hide my shame.

I turn my head when I feel her hand grab my biceps.

"Etts fighne—eyem okay," she says softly as our eyes meet.

Even though I don't understand her strange language, I understand her intent.

No harm caused.

I am astounded by her ability to soothe the agitated brothers. I can sense their desire to reach out and pull at her delicate frame, but I can also perceive their self-restraint, which is a sensation I have never experienced before.

I wonder if her mating mark has anything to do with their sudden obedience. The thought of her mark brings the old familiar ache back, the wanting to belong to someone completely. If this truly is my path, if Leeenuh is my future, maybe completing the Great Proving will somehow cement our bond. Even if I don't bear a mating mark of my own.

Leeenuh sits next to the dried plants and twists the lashings into cords. I watch her, longingly, as the ache roots itself deeper into my heart. What was that strange custom she initiated—the act of pressing our lips together? The Andjin have no such tradition, and I don't know what it's supposed to signify.

My body reacted…interestingly.

Before I turn back to her, I flip my still hard cock up into the wrap's waistband before I make my way over to sit by Leeenuh.

Grabbing the dried seaweed, I begin to work on her restraints. I open my mouth a few times, but the right words won't come out. Leeenuh must notice my anxiety.

"Kitaico, doan worree abou eet," she says, patting me on the back.

She holds up one of the purple torun sponges for just a moment as our fingers touch, and I show her the knots I planned on using.

Even though we're from different worlds, Leeenuh is a quick study. I grapple with the impossibility of our situation as we work side by side. I can't help but let my mind wander, to imagine what my life would be like if we were *true mates*.

I could love Leeenuh. I know there's a connection beyond her mating mark between us. Is it possible that my role in her life could be more than that of just a protector? Could she even want me in that way?

A brief flash of her with a round belly lounging in my nest crosses my mind. I feed her the tenderest bits of my kill, and she lets me ornament her body with the jeweled body chains given to expectant mothers.

She presses our mouths together again and smiles at me.

But I scrub the imaginary life from my mind.

Leeenuh doesn't want me as her mate, and I will keep her safe and respect her choices.

I snap back from my daydreams as one of the brothers slips around Leeenuh's back and begins to creep up her thigh.

"Guud boi," she tells him before stroking him softly. She doesn't remove him, and a tingling sensation shoots from her hand on my foretentacle to my already aching cock. I can feel precum leaking from my tip and have to bite the inside of my cheek to stifle a moan.

I wonder if I've offended the Great Mother in a past life to be tortured like this. Maybe I haven't given enough of myself to this great test. I am not the strongest hopeful in my division, or the cleverest. I am just Kitaico, a normal male of no great importance.

Is devoting myself to Leeenuh part of my Proving?

Is resisting her my ultimate test?

9 /
a caring gesture

I KISSED *him because I needed to distract him*, I remind myself. As much as the brothers aren't under his control, they're still part of his body. I figured a shock to the system might get them to release me.

I turn my head to him as we sit side by side, wrapping the cords meant to tie me down for my next heat. He flicks his tongue past the sharp point of his fang in some gesture of concentration. I remember being surprised at how gentle the kiss was with a mouth as intimidating as his.

I kissed him to calm things down, right?

His face was shocked when I finally pulled away. There was something else behind the shock that I had a harder time reading, too—maybe just confusion about what the hell I was even doing to him.

Most alien species don't kiss, some even find it insulting or unsanitary. Before the war on the Deenz, they kept us in more centralized bunkhouse stations when we were off rotation. The other girls were at the same Deenz station as my group of bubble dancers that first night.

Trembling with fear, exhausted from endless tears in my cramped bunk, I cautiously eavesdropped on their hushed conversation. An older woman was giving one of the new brothel girls the ins and outs of the game. She was running over a list of the few species that kissed in space. It was short, and she had warned the girl that some aliens might even hurt her if she attempted it.

I remember being glad that I wasn't in her position, that all I had to do was dance.

At least Kitaico didn't look disgusted with my gesture.

And the kiss worked, didn't it? The brothers released me, and I think they're even listening to me now…as weird as it is to say. One of them, the left tentacle, sits on my thigh like a house cat. I slide my hand over him, thinking the occasional pet can't hurt, can it?

My hand strokes up the appendage, feeling the texture of the skin that sits over the rippling muscular tube. It's not as soft as my skin, but it feels like a well-worn piece of leather. Thick and pliable with lots of give. I absentmindedly let my hands trace a bit higher, wrapping my fingers around his tentacle. My fingers don't touch as I attempt to close them around the girthy tube, and I slide a hand down its length.

As my palm moves against it, Kitaico stiffens.

"Leeenuh," he whispers.

"Yeah?" I ask, rubbing small circles over the tentacle's tip in my lap.

"I–I assume you do not understand, and I do n-not wish to embarrass you…" Kitaico stutters, stumbling a bit over his words. "But if you continue to caress my foretentacles, I will need to be excused to finish the job myself. Such touches make my cock throb with an intensity I don't think I've ever known before." His eyes darken as they meet my own.

My hands fly up into the air, dropping the brother in my lap.

As if ungrateful for losing my touch, the tentacle winds its way up my wrist and pulls my hand back down.

"I didn't know you could feel them…which, now that I'm saying that out loud, sounds so incredibly stupid," I mutter, pushing the tentacle out of my lap.

"Thank you," Kitaico says with a sigh of relief. "I don't expect you to know much about my people, as I know little about the humans, either." He focuses his hungry eyes on his work, knotting the cord over the purple alien sea sponges.

"Can I ask you what you did earlier? When you pressed your mouth against mine?" he tries to say nonchalantly.

So, he's still thinking about the kiss, too.

"Oh, that was a kiss," I tell him, bringing my pointer and middle finger to my lips.

"Kisth," he says softly. "What does it signify?"

What does a kiss mean? The question spins in my mind. God, what, doesn't it? I've kissed in moments of pure joy, the taste of laughter lingering on my lips. I've kissed in moments of grief when the tears mingled with the bittersweet touch. And in moments of unbound rage, a collision of lips instead of fists. But as I gaze into his eyes, I sense he's not seeking the meaning of any ordinary kiss. He wants to understand what *our kiss* truly meant.

Was it only to catch him off guard?

When Kitaico wasn't here earlier, I panicked. For better or worse, he's now my protector—and I think I wanted to kiss him.

"A kiss is a sign of affection," I tell him, unsure how to mime out that sentiment.

Putting my hand over my heart, I tilt my head and make an "aw" noise, hoping there's some universal understanding.

Kitaico's eyes drift back to my own, his brow cocked.

"Indigestion?" he asks.

I stifle a laugh and shake my head no. I look at the giant confused alien and open my arms.

"Can I hug you?" I ask him.

He might not understand me, but he leans closer, and I wrap my arms around his back, rubbing along his spine.

With a slight pause, he inhales sharply before settling his chin on the top of my head. Sitting on the floor of the cave, our contrasting heights are starkly evident.

"This is the same as a kisth?" His breath fans over my hair.

I nod, still holding my arms around him.

"Care. A kisth is for those you care about?" he says, wrapping his arms around my body, copying the movements of my hands on his back.

"Yes," I breathe, his touch doing more to my senses than I want to admit to myself.

"If that is the case," he says, pulling back and tilting my chin up with his hand, "let me return the gesture."

A slow, agonizing buzz resonates in my ears as Kitaico leans in, his lips meeting mine with deliberate slowness. As our bodies turn against each other, I can taste the salty tang of the ocean on his lips. As he withdraws his hand from my chin, his fingertips gently glide through my hair. He presses harder into me, his foretentacles grabbing my hips.

Sparks ignite at my core, a sensation so different from the heat his venom once brought. This isn't a frenzy. My body yearns for this. It wants Kitaico—I want him to go further.

His tongue tangles with my own, and he moans into my mouth as the foretentacles lift me to straddle his hips. The strength shouldn't shock me, but it's as if I weigh nothing when they move me. It makes me realize that the brothers and Kitaico have shown incredible restraint.

I can feel the throbbing of his cock and the pulsating of his surrounding tentacles through the thin woven wrap he wears at his waist. I can feel myself growing slick and ready for him.

But just as I'm waiting for him to move us further toward what feels like inevitable sex, he breaks the kiss, and his camouflage shuffles through several colors before returning to his yellow. Kitaico lifts me off his laps and sets me down chastely next to him.

"I'm sorry, the brothers get ahead of themselves. A kisth is a much more intimate sign of caring than the Andjin have." He smiles at me before picking up his ropes again. "Thank you for sharing that with me."

Oh.

I pick up the dried seaweed too, not knowing what else to do as my brain lacks the blood flow my pussy does.

This has all escalated so fucking quickly.

I twist the rope tighter than I ever have twisted anything in my life. These restraints better work because I will climb Kitaico like a tree once the heat hits.

"You're welcome," I say, a little salty, but of course, the sweet alien doesn't pick up on my annoyed tone. He's far too kind to assume the worst of me.

fingerpaints

THE KISS MADE THINGS AWKWARD, there's no way around that fact. So, in classic Midwestern fashion, I push those awkward feelings down and act as if nothing is bothering me.

But since we're both sequestered in this not very large cave, there's only so much we can do to stay out of each other's hair.

Kitaico and I made all the rope we'd need for the restraints, and the rest of the work has been up to him. He stands on the bed, gently chiseling little channels into the ceiling to thread the ropes through.

I've tidied what little there is to be tidied, I've slept as much as possible, and if I never bundle up another dried fish again, it'll be too soon. I guess the cabin fever wouldn't be so bad if I wasn't also trying to deny my attraction to Kitaico. Even if it's only a chemical response, it's starting to feel *real*.

I sit near the store shelves and watch his rippling back as he angles the tool to continue his chipping. His ass flexes as he goes onto tiptoes. My brain conjures up an image of him pumping his bizarre tentacle- surrounded cock into me, thrusting deep.

I bite the inside of my cheek, dropping my eyes but hopefully picking my brain up out of the gutter. In my lap lays a rounded shell full of the purple nuite fruit. Its dark purple juice stains my fingertips, but it tastes so much better than the salty fish jerky that I eat a lot of it. It's tangy, kind of a cross between a plum and a grape. It would make a killer pie.

Do aliens even have pie?

I mean, I shouldn't complain either way, it's so much tastier than the grey sludge the Deenz would feed me. The porridge I ate as a bubble babe was nutrient dense, I'm sure, but devoid of flavor.

Seems a silly thing to be concerned about when you've been abducted by aliens, but I would have dreams about fried cheese curds and chili dogs. For weeks, I'd crave nothing but the greasiest dive bar food.

Eventually though, you get too tired to dream. You wake up, dance in a plastic bubble for whatever alien species is on the docket that day, eat your mush, sleep, and repeat.

Human women are an investment for my previous captors, and I still can't figure out why they dumped my pod here. Maybe I wasn't worth the cost anymore? Had I aged out of bubble dancing?

I'm not even sure how long I'd been away from Earth, maybe months? The last birthday party I had I was thirty-two. Absent-mindedly I run my fingers down the side of my face, searching for new wrinkles. Anything to prove the passage of time.

"Leeenuh, that'll stain," Kitaico mutters, grabbing a rough woven cloth and dipping it into the small pool of water he's been staring at this morning.

I think it's the first words he's spoken to me since the kiss, days ago.

When he comes over, he swipes the purple juice from my cheek with a grin. His fingertips linger, and his skin flashes purple for just a second.

My breath catches, and I can't help but lean into his hand

before embarrassment gets the better of me and I shake off his touch.

"Oh yeah, sorry, I knew that," I say, ignoring the heat in my chest as he touches me.

"You alright?" he asks tepidly, hand still floating in the air where it once held my face.

Does he want us to talk about the kiss?

He's hovering over me in a way that lets me know he's got something on his mind.

I nod quickly, standing to walk to the other side of the room. Distance makes it easier to not stare into his kind eyes and not get butterflies low in my belly. Feelings I thought I wouldn't feel ever again.

We both need something to do, I realize as I lean my hand up against the wall, trying my best to act casual.

Kitaico grimaces and sighs, pointing to my hand.

"It'll stain the wall too, Leeenuh," he sighs, bringing the rag over to me again.

"Geez, sorry, my head's not really in the right place," I ramble as if he can understand me.

I take the cloth from him and rub my fingers clean. I try to rub my fingerprints off the wall, but the porous rock surface just soaks up the juice on contact. I scrub harder, knowing it's not going to make a difference.

"It's alright Leeenuh, it's kind of unavoidable to not stain something when you eat nuite fruit—it's one of our most popular dyes," he says with those same kind eyes I've been avoiding.

God, my insides must be stained purple by now if I've been eating dye. But if it'll stain the wall, that gives me an idea.

"Kitaico, do you care if I…" I realize I'm going to have to show him, and I run back and grab the shell full of fruit. I dip my finger into the purple sap and hover it over the rocks before looking back at him.

"You want to mark the wall?" he asks with a cocked brow.

I nod and point to my many tattoos, then back to the wall.

"Oh, you want to draw on the wall?" He grins when I nod again.

"Whatever you want, Leeenuh, if it'll make you happy," he says sweetly.

I'm almost distracted enough to not notice him grabbing one of the brothers and holding it against his thigh as it reaches for me.

I want him to touch me, to soothe this itch I feel building inside me, one that I know only he can scratch.

Maybe it wouldn't be so bad if he helped me during my next heat?

I dip my finger again, bringing it up to the wall and making short strokes. Back at my studio, I wasn't known for portraits. I was the girl you went to for nautical scenes and underwater creatures. You'd be shocked at the number of landlocked Midwesterners with turtle and dolphin tattoos.

But there's something I miss more than cheese dogs and chili curds, and that's my grandmother.

Yeah, that's it, let's just get incredibly sad about never seeing the woman who raised you again to avoid horny thoughts. Great job, Lena.

But, it kind of does work. Because I'm using my finger, I stick to a more impressionistic style, broader strokes to give the impression of detail.

I start with her Ukrainian nose, strong and beautiful, and let that flow into defining her eyes.

Even though I can feel Kitaico staring a hole in my back, I let myself get wrapped up in this giant portrait. I flick my pinky, creating one set of crow's feet before moving to the other. Her round face comes next, framed by her soft gray bob.

I forgot how much I missed art.

"Who is this?" His curious voice ponders behind me as I work.

I pause, realizing I don't know how to mime the word for grandmother. I turn to him, with my purple fingers pointing to my chest.

"My…" I set the bowl down on the ground and use both my hands to round out my belly. "Mother's mother?"

Kitaico's face goes blank, and he coughs, looking away.

I cradle an imaginary baby with one arm while pointing back and forth between me and the baby.

"Oh, your mother?" His eyes light up.

Close enough, especially since I never really knew my real mother or father.

"Yeah." I nod.

He turns back to the painting, rough and unfinished but still recognizable as my grandmother.

"She seems wise," he says thoughtfully.

"She would love to hear that." I can't help but chuckle. She was a real *her way or the highway type.* "God, do I miss her."

I barely notice the tear falling down my cheek until Kitaico is there, swiping it away. We're so close that I can hear the dueling rhythm of our heartbeats.

"Do you miss her?" he asks, his breath fanning on the side of my face as he tilts his head.

"More than anything," I sniffle.

"I'm sorry. It's not the same, but I miss my family too. The males are taken from their homes to be raised together as hopefuls. I haven't seen my mother in many years."

I want to ask him what a hopeful is, but I don't know if I have the willpower to step back and explain it using gestures.

"Would a kiss help?" His tentacle touches my hip, pulling me closer.

Help, hell no. Would it make me too horny to function? You betcha.

I put my hand on his chest, pushing him gently away.

"No." I shake my head with a forced smile. I don't want him to think I don't appreciate the gesture, but I need some time to think about what all this means. I push him back against the lone stool until he sits.

Distract him, he needs it as much as I do.

I turn back to the wall and begin to paint next to my grandmother's portrait.

I look over at him, trying to understand his proportions and adapting them to my knowledge of human anatomy. His tentacles, especially the longer ones, are super fun to render in this medium. The appendages' width is as wide as my thumb and made with grand sweeping motions.

I rough out his eyes, glancing back and forth between him and the art, and see his smile grow.

"That's me!" he says in a wave of pure excitement only someone as genuine as him could pull off. "You're perfect."

I smile, knowing that this isn't really my best work, but accept the compliment all the same.

"You should see what I can do with a needle and skin," I laugh as I continue to paint.

11 /
a great honor

IT'S BEEN days since I shared the kiss with Leeenuh, and I can't stop thinking about how she felt against me.

I tie off one restraint to an anchor point in the craggy ceiling. I get a bit of the bioluminescent dust on my hands as I do and wipe it on my bare chest. Pulling the rope to test its strength, I slide back onto my knees into the nest. My body weight doesn't threaten to break the rope, so I'm satisfied with my work.

Leeenuh has been waiting patiently for me to rig everything up. She inspects everything with squinted eyes before shrugging and sitting down on the bed next to me.

We've gotten into a routine as we ready ourselves for her next heat. When we wake, I prepare food and Leeenuh uses the relief hole and brushes through her fine mane before splashing fresh water on her face and rubbing her body down with one of the torun sponges.

Her grooming habits are always interesting to watch, especially as she cares for her mane. She's told me it's called hairuh, but it reminds me of the Fi'len mane. The Fi'len rule the planet that the Korlyan Moon orbits. Their heads are crowned similar to Leeenuh's, but unlike hers, they don't hold water.

When she wets her mane, it's soaked for hours.

We mainly work on the restraints, or she helps me with storing and sorting the dried dredlin. Then sleep and repeat. I won't pretend that resisting her isn't a challenge, but even in the midst of mundane tasks, I'm pleased to be in her presence.

But there's always an edge, a line I know I cannot cross. I don't know if her heat approaches or if I'm just being driven mad when I think her scent is stronger, more enticing than before. I stare at her body. Even Leeenuh's breasts seem fuller than yesterday.

Leeenuh has been agitated since late last night. She fidgets constantly in her sleep in the nest while I rest in the tidal pool meant for my future children's nursery. I know the basics of matehood, that I will rut my female until her belly is swollen with my young, but there's so much I feel unprepared for.

"It will hold," I tell her confidently, because I know it will. I'm glad of it, as I have no desire for Leeenuh to injure herself as badly as she did before. She nods, shifting uncomfortably next to me.

"Eye tink twodaay's da daay." She speaks her strange human words as she wiggles in her seat. I might not understand her completely, but I know what she's trying to convey.

I move all the faster on my last knot, pulling it taut against the ceiling before stepping back to admire my work.

"I think it's ready for you," I tell her with a nod before reaching for her hand as she steps up onto the nest platform. Her fingers feel like fire entwined with mine, and I swear I can feel the mating mark on her palm burning into my own. I release her hand reluctantly as she kneels, holding the rope up to her wrist and looking at me with a pleading face.

"Oh, of course I'll help you." I hop up next to her. I grab her small beige wrist and wrap the padded portion of the restraint around it. Looping the rope, I truss it tightly.

"Is that okay?" I ask, finding it hard to keep my concentration on the task at hand. When I lean over her to secure her other wrist, I can smell her cunt and the dampness pooling there.

I know the wrap I wear does little to hide my quickly thickening cock, but I don't want to make her feel awkward. She can't control the heat any more than I can control my body's reaction to it. This entire situation feels like a punishment for which I wish I knew my crimes.

"Kitaico…" Leeenuh starts, biting in her lip in a way that doesn't help my throbbing cock's situation.

"What is it, Leeenuh?" I double check my work before moving onto her ankle. "It's not uncomfortable, is it?"

"Noe, noe, it's feyena. Eye jus wan two leht ewe no, that eye no dis is hard four ewe two, and that eyem ought so unfeelin that eye down't si dat…eye jus wan two sayay that eye down't myend if ewe, ewe no, elp yourself out if ewe nead two." She's rambling, and a pink color blooms on her cheeks and chest.

I swear once my translator chip is reactivated, I'll never let them turn it off again.

"I don't understand. Can you show me?"

Any color drains from those high cheekbones as she blanches a sickly white. With a quick burst of air through her nostrils, she sets her jaw in some kind of determination.

"Kitaico." She points to me before pointing at my cock and then at her own cunt. She shakes her head. "No sex."

I'm briefly hurt. Does she think I've forgotten her wishes? That I'm not better than an animal and would rut her as soon as the heat takes over? I would never do that, even if I'd love nothing more than to feel her clasping around my cock.

"I know Leeenuh, don't worry, I am no brute!" I will keep my word with no hesitation.

"No, no. It's okuh if Kitaico tikes caruh of imself," she says as she points to my cock and mimes what is very much the universal sign for jacking off. Her voice wobbles less as she continues. "In act, it's okuh if kitaico touches leeenuh, to elp wit heat. Jus no alien peen inside mi, okuh?"

"Surely I'm mistaken in my understanding," I say, hope welling in my chest. "Do you want me to touch myself and touch you?"

"It ould ache meye heat easier eye tink, to ave ewe touch mi," she whispers. She takes my foretentacle, already sitting in her lap, and puts it over her covered mound.

"Okuh two touch wit tentickles"—she reaches for my hand— "an hand." But when she motions to my dick, she shakes her head no again.

"We can touch, but not mate?" My voice cracks.

She nods her head enthusiastically. I'm not sure if she's excited to have gotten her point across, or excited at the prospect of what might happen now.

Maybe it's a little of both.

"Are you sure?" I ask, still dubious. "Your heat hasn't started yet, has it?"

I know the answer is no, that there will be no denying it when the heat takes hold.

"Eyem ure, it's okuh." She smiles and slides her unbound ankle to me.

Leeenuh wants me to touch her, to give us both pleasure.

My skin ripples through several different shades before settling on a deep purple. I gulp down whatever anxiety I have about this situation back into my belly.

"If this is what you wish, I will not deny you such things as my mate." I try to keep my voice as cool as I can, but my body sings with the prospect of being able to touch her, to help her through her heat.

By the Great Mother's hand, it would be my honor. My smart little Leeenuh has found a loophole. If we aren't actually mating, surely I am allowed to touch. This is by her request after all, and all I want to do is make her more comfortable.

Once her ankles are bound, I hop down from the nest platform.

"Are you ready?"

When she nods, I pull gently on the lead rope until her arms raise over her head. I watch her for any signs of discomfort or distress but find none. I continue until her hands can no longer reach the tender parts of her sex. They've healed well, but we can't risk her injuring herself again.

"Comfortable enough?" I ask my little mate as she flexes and tests our system. When she nods, I pull a stool up and sit near the nest. Admiring my work.

Viewing her plush body, I decide I was right. Her breasts are more swollen, their new fullness has my eyes lingering longer than might be considered polite. The way her nipples peak through her thin blue top makes me throb. I wish she had put my mouth on the list of acceptable touches. I want so badly to taste her skin. The smell of it is intoxicating enough.

As she sighs impatiently and fidgets to get comfortable, inspiration suddenly hits me with a great idea.

"Maybe, since touches are okay, I could touch you to bring on your heat, and we could end it sooner?" I ask, my heart in my throat, waiting for her response.

She cocks her head. "Ight bee smart," she gets out somewhat cautiously and nods. "Is okuh."

I smile confidently, but I know the shaking of my hand betrays me as I reach up toward her perfect breast. When I place my palm over its warmth, Leeenuh closes her eyes and mewls softly.

"You tell me what feels good, so I'll know what you actually like before the heat takes hold—tell me what to do if it's not good for you."

She nods, arching her chest into my hand. I softly pinch the nipple before trailing my fingers down to the wrap around her waist.

I can smell her cunt readying itself for rutting. My cock

jumps when I put my hand on the knot that holds the skirts in place against her hips.

"Can I remove this?" I murmur, not wanting to scare her.

She opens her eyes, boring into my soul with hooded lids, and nods.

When I tug the knot and drop her skirt, it slides down her ample hips and decorated skin. I can't help but pull her scent greedily into my nose. Her mound, covered with hairuh, shines and drips.

I rub my hands together, afraid that my skin might not match the searing heat I feel coming off her sex. I cup the pink lips of her cunt, hopefully letting her adjust to my touch.

I know I can continue when I feel her weight shift into my palm, as if she's giving herself to me. I take my middle finger, pulling a bead of her wetness from her opening up across the little knob of flesh that sits at the apex of her slit.

As I trace over the bump with my fingers, she lets out a delicious little moan.

"Good?" I ask her, enjoying this little pleasure button between her legs.

"Fuuc, yis," she pants. "Moor."

One brother snakes up over my shoulder and coils around her back, threading under her armpit and settling to massage and grip her breast.

"Kitaico..." she breathes, throwing her head back and sagging against the restraints.

"You are so slick even before the heat, Leeenuh. You need this relief. Let me make you feel good," I say before testing her depth, dipping my finger into her entrance.

I was right, she would milk my cock so well. The muscles along her inner walls flutter over my single digit. They pulse harder as I add a second finger.

"You're such a sweet mate, so ready to be rutted," I whisper, unable to control myself, letting the fantasy of her underneath me eclipse my reality.

"I need to touch myself, Leeenuh. You're too good, too perfect not to," I tell her before grabbing myself at the root.

Her eyes open and she stares at my painfully hard cock. The tentacles of my mating crest grasp over my hand and I work my length. Her eyes sear into me as I stroke my length and I slide out of her. My fingers, slick with her juices, find the delicate pearl nestled at the apex of her cunt.

I watch her face intently, allowing myself to be enthralled with the pleasure I'm giving her, that I barely notice the other brother notching himself at her entrance.

Only when she whimpers my name do I realize the brother is already inside her, thrusting into her warm depths.

"You feel so good," I say. "Tell me if you want me to stop. I swear to the Great Mother that I will."

She bucks against my hand as my foretentcle pumps into her. Even though I can't control it, I can feel what he feels. I almost gasp when the rush of wetness slides from her cunt and down the length of the tentacle.

"Down't ewe daruh staph," she moans.

With her demands, I know Leeenuh's heat has officially begun.

As I work her pearl, the muscles inside her grasp at my fingers. Her hips buck faster as she searches for release. I know I'll do whatever it takes to give it to her.

"What do you need, Leenuh?" I ask through gritted teeth, trying my hardest not to spill before she finds her own pleasure.

Her wild eyes shoot open and dart to my leaking cock.

"Uck mi, put dat thuick dic deep insiduh mi," she begs.

She wants me to rut her into submission...but that's just the heat talking.

"Just touches, remember? Just the brothers and my hand."

We cannot mate, this pleasure for us both won't disqualify me from the Proving. I won't dishonor her by mating her without being worthy of such a beauty.

"Moor, jus moar then puhlease!" she pleads.

As if they can understand her, the brother on her breast slides between her legs. While the other limb pumps in and out of her, making obscene wet sounds as it does, the remaining tentacle slides into Leeenuh's dripping cunt as well.

She gasps as it works in slowly, fighting the motion of its twin, until it stretches her hole wide. She lets out a guttural noise when the brother tests its new surroundings, prodding the denser flesh of her channel, pushing toward her belly.

My hand clasps over the head of my cock, trying desperately to keep my seed in.

My fingers on her sensitive nub don't relent as the tentacles fuck, filling her cunt completely. Even from the front, I can see the glorious muscles of her ass clench. Leeenuh shudders as the wave of ecstasy rolls through her. She clamps over my tentacles, and they continue to fuck her all while I feel my balls tighten. Streams of her hot liquid squirt out with every thrust. I'm past the point of no return when I come apart.

I have to steady myself against Leeenuh as I fear I might black out, her thighs having long since snapped shut over my hand. It's as if my touch is too much for her to handle.

"Kitaico, Kitaico," she begs for something as she's slack in her restraints. A sheen of perspiration dews on her perfect body.

When the tunneling on my vision ends and I finally remove my hand from her between her legs, I realize what she wants.

"Moor," she moans, arching her hips toward me, begging for my hand.

The brothers haven't stopped their work, and if anything, they fuck her cunt harder.

Who am I to deny my mate?

i can't promise you that

WHEN I COME TO, I can already tell that my body isn't wrecked like I was after the first heat. Sure, I'm pleasantly sore, but I don't feel like I've dragged my pussy across a rough carpet all night.

I feel kind of, I don't know, good? Maybe relaxed is the better word.

Though my ankles and wrists are still secured, the restraints are looser than they were last night. I lie toward the top edge of the bed while his body is opposite mine. I cast my eyes down to where Kitaico sleeps, curled around my thighs. His yellow head rests on my lap while the brothers wrap around my middle in some kind of protective hold.

He looks exhausted as he lies on his back. His once engorged dick is tucked behind the tentacles that surround it.

It might be strange, but I'm weirdly proud of the fact that we're covered in his release, the faint purple streaking both our bellies. I enjoyed myself, but should I have? Is it wrong to find pleasure from each other when I know he wants more?

I think I wanted to give him a bit of happiness, like a reward. Fuck me if he didn't earn it. As if him giving me my release is some antidote to the heat's brain fog, I can remember most of what took place last night—and most of those memories are of multiple orgasms.

His foretentacles stroke along my breast as if they're not really awake, and Kitaico fidgets in his sleep.

As the brothers work my nipples, I'm brought back to when they were plunging into me. When I said he could touch me with his tentacles and hands, I didn't think about his tentacles penetrating me—but I won't pretend I didn't like it.

They worked me in absolutely delicious ways that I'm not sure a cock could. I clench the muscles of my sex as I think about how they coiled inside me. One of the brothers fucked me senseless, while the other stroked my G-spot until I squirted.

I can say, with complete confidence, that I was convinced squirting wasn't something I could do. Until last night, no other male, human or alien, has ever made me feel like Kitaico did.

But for as good as it was, I could tell we both wanted more. In the haze of the heat, I wanted him to fuck me. Something primal inside me wanted him to ignore my rules and to fuck me until his cum leaked down my thighs.

Just the thought of his purple seed dripping down my legs has heat pooling at my core. I'm not sure where the fuck this newfound breeding kink is coming from, but I'd put my money on the heat-inducing venom still pulsing through my veins.

Kitaico groans, arching his back and pulling in a deep breath. As the air hits his lungs, his eyes shoot open. He blinks rapidly, attempting to clear the sleep from his vision.

"Did I sleep so long it's already time for your next heat?" he asks in a panic.

"What? No...Why on earth would you think that?" I ask before I feel the tiny bead of wetness drip down my thigh.

Oh, because he can probably smell you getting turned on.

Shaking my head no, I press my thighs together, hoping to conceal the aroma I'm sure he's already smelled.

Kitaico turns to me, tilting his head and cocking a brow as he examines my face.

"You certainly don't seem as enthusiastic as you did earlier… despite how good you smell." He rushes the last part out as he stands. His once soft cock seems to be reacting to my scent as it bulges past the swath of tentacles.

"Thank you for allowing me that…that experience last night, Leeenuh. I will treasure it always," he whispers as he leans over me, his arms reaching for my bound wrist.

"No problem." I gulp, keeping myself from letting his mere presence arouse me any further.

I think unsexy thoughts as he frees my first wrist. Baseball, the way my Great-Aunt Mildred's house smelled, *Old Yeller*, algebra…

"If you'll allow it, I think adding my tongue to the list of things allowed to pleasure you would be very good for both of us." Kitaico's breath fans over my neck as he unties my other hand.

"Oh, yeah sure, totally…" Imagining his tongue on my pussy is not helping this situation at all.

He pulls back, trying to grasp what I'm saying.

"Would that be alright, Leeenuh?" Kitaico asks in earnest.

I can't meet his gaze, so I cast my eyes down and nod. I hate the blush spreading from my chest to my cheeks.

If he's as good with his tongue as he was with his other limbs, I might not be able to wait until the next heat.

When my wrists are both free, I wrap the blanket tightly around my shoulders. I take a deep breath and let the thought I just had hit me.

Am I fucking hot for Kitaico, beyond the venom?

Do I want more than sex with the bizarre, thoughtful, attractive, tentacled alien that is stretching in front of me now?

I wrack my brain for any inkling of this being from a chemical reaction from the sting or something more.

Kitaico pads over to the other side of the cave to the "shower," flexing the sinewy muscles of his sides, and letting the water hit his rock-hard abdominal muscles. He tilts his chin back, splashing the water over his face and through the tentacles on his head. He rubs his hand over the dried purple remnants of his cum on his stomach, washing the evidence of our time together back into the ocean beyond the relief hole.

My chest tightens and I suddenly feel as though I'm spying on Kitaico. It's not like getting me off wasn't intimate, but there's something telling me that to look at him now is wrong.

Maybe I should look away, but for as intimate as his actions are, it doesn't feel like I shouldn't be part of them. My mouth parts, and I breathe a little heavier as he grips his cock and pushes the last bit of leaking seed from its tip. He steps out, shaking the water from his head's tentacles before he catches me gawking at him.

"Oh, I'm sorry, I should have offered this to you first." He frowns. "Would you like to clean up?"

I nod and rush over to where the alien Adonis stands, still dripping with water.

I didn't think that the water wasn't going to be warm, and I rush into the steady stream that falls down the cave's wall. I yelp as it makes contact with my skin, the cold causing the hairs on my body to stand on end.

Before I have time to adjust, Kitaico's arms and the brothers wrap tightly around me, shielding me from the chill of the makeshift shower.

"It's cold, I thought you knew." He chuckles as I shiver. "Deep breaths, Leeenuh."

He still absorbs the brunt of the cold water as he runs his hands over the bottom of my belly. Kitaico splashes more of the water over my skin to remove the purple marks he left there last night.

I wish they would dip lower, I wish he would—

"I could arrange for a hot bath tonight, if you think you're up for it?" He says softly as he works his fingers into my hair and massages the nape of my neck until I'm slumping against his firm chest. "We'd have to travel a short distance to the surface, but I'm confident it will be quick enough that your human lungs won't struggle."

A head massage? A warm bath?

Maybe it's not the venom…maybe Kitaico is just a fucking gem.

"Yes." I nod, letting myself sag further back into him, the tension of my neck muscles melting away.

"I like taking care of you, you know," he whispers as he guides me away from the water, grabbing a fresh woven blanket and shimmying it over my body to dry me. He spins me to face him, rubbing the cloth over my hair.

When Kitaico pushes my hair back, he lets down his usual polite facade. His eyes are intense, and they darken as he speaks. "Even if I never bear your mating mark, this could be enough. I would devote myself to you, Leeenuh."

"Oh," is all my brain can get together.

Is that what I want?

I want to fuck him, I know that.

"I can't promise you that, Kitaico." My voice cracks. "I like you…but this situation is fucked. You're so much kinder than the Deenz, but I might need some breathing room before I commit to anything long term." It pains me to be honest, even if I know he can't understand me.

His brows knit in confusion—for Chrissakes, I can't even communicate to him properly.

If he's implying what I think he's proposing, it hits me one thousand times harder than the cold water. Forever, in a cave, with albeit a delightful alien gentleman, isn't how my story is supposed to go.

"Go slower," I say, my hands raised and pushing him away

slightly. "We'll talk"—I mime my hands speaking to each other —"once your translator chip is turned back on."

I bring my finger to his head and tap where I think his chip would be, where it is on me, at least.

"I'm sorry." He plays it off as though he didn't just offer to dedicate his life to me, wraps me in the towel, and turns back to his stores as though he's looking for something.

"God, don't be sorry, Kitaico. You deserve someone better than a lost bubble babe, someone who can give you what you want. A real mate." I put my hand on his shoulder.

He covers my hand with his own and looks back at me.

"What is it?" he asks.

"Never mind." I place an apologetic kiss on his fingers. I can feel him freeze as my lips touch his skin—its patterns shift to a deep purple that creeps up his arm.

There's no way to mime the conflict I feel about the sweet alien right now. This conversation is going to have to wait.

I shuffle to the other side of the cave, sitting next to the shallow pool that Kitaico normally sleeps in. I trace my fingers through the teal water, my mating mark tingling as I do.

For as good as he makes me feel, and as well as he treats me, maybe we're just too different.

There's a part of me holding onto the idea that one day I might be able to go home—which feels like a delusion after hearing about the few girls who escaped the Deenz. Earth is off-limits for everyone but the alien hivemind that trafficked me here.

I glance over my shoulder to see Kitaico staring at me before he quickly looks away.

Maybe if I had any control over my life and how I ended up here, it would be different. I could give him what he wants, and I could give in to these feelings that are rooting deep inside of me.

Maybe.

splish splash, it's an alien bath

I NEED to get to the capital, Great Proving or not. I don't know if I can let Leeenuh go after what happened between us last night. Even if I'm not her mate, my venom flows through her…it must mean something. This can't just be a coincidence that this perfect goddess fell into my lap. There's no way the Great Mother didn't have a hand in the situation.

It's not Leeenuh's fault that she's unsure of me. I haven't proven myself yet. She might not know the Andjin traditions, but what have I shown her except my own debauchery?

What kind of male accidentally stings an unwitting female?

If we get back to the capital, I'll have the chance to prove myself to her and my people.

I can show Leeenuh that there is no one on the Korlyan Moon that will treasure her more than I will.

I push my hurt aside, focusing on the task at hand—caring for the female bearing my mating mark.

"If you still want that bath, I can make preparations," I say nonchalantly, glancing at Leeenuh.

She smiles a slow smile before nodding.

"Excellent, we'll eat, and I'll show you the hot springs."

Leeenuh gnaws at the dried dredlin with her blunt little teeth. I wish I had more variety for her and kick myself for not thinking that my future mate might like something else. I should have thought to acquire sustenance beyond the most hardy of stored food.

She struggles as she chews but doesn't complain. I wonder what her life might have been like before she literally sank into mine. That's one thing I can't wait to talk to her about when my translator chip is restored. Right now, I'm enjoying spending time with the strange little alien who is my mate.

She seems to have perked up at my mention of a bath, though. I think getting out to the nest and to the hot springs would do us both good. As much as I don't mind this newfound closeness the two of us have fostered, I don't want to smother her with my attentions.

If Leeenuh had her way, she would never let me fuss over her. There's something so bizarre about a mate wanting to do things for herself. I guess the Andjin culture expects males to dote, but I can't imagine a human not wanting to do the same for the vision sitting in front of me.

"Yur stairing et mi," she says with a raised brow.

I just tilt my head and appraise her more intently, unsure of what she said.

"Whenever you're full, we can head out—the cave's entrance isn't too far from the surface, and the hot springs aren't much farther than that."

With a finger pointed at the cave ceiling, Leeenuh holds her breath and directs her gaze toward me. She flaps her hands as if she's swimming and then places them at her throat in a mock drowning.

"Oh, how long you'd need to hold your breath? I can breathe for you, don't worry," I reassure her.

"Eef eets naught far, maybi eye shuud prakteetce? Eye allwaze won et olding meye breauth et da layke." She frowns.

The more comfortable Leeenuh has gotten here, the more I see her stubborn side. She doesn't like anyone to do something for her that she thinks she can do herself.

It's so incredibly endearing that I want to wrap her up in my limbs and never let her go, my headstrong human.

"Why don't I check how long it takes, then?" I ask, pointing to the nest's door.

Leeenuh nods, looking relieved to have gotten her message across.

"I'll be right back. Never fear, my Leeenuh!"

Rushing to the opening, I dive through and start counting.

One, two, three, four…

I kick my legs as my ascent starts.

Ten, eleven, twelve, thirteen…

Dredlin scales flick past me like starlight, and I push my arms up and out.

Twenty-five, twenty-six, twenty-seven…

I weave through some flotsam being pushed down to the sea floor by the currents.

Forty, forty-one, forty-two…

I can see the light refracting from the surface of the water now, not much farther.

Fifty-five!

I break through the surface and scan the horizon for danger. Once I'm satisfied that everything appears normal, I dive much more quickly back into the nest. As I pop through the opening, Leeenuh gawks at me.

"Dat seams furthur dan ewe tink it iz…" she mutters under her breath.

"You'll only need to hold your breath for a count of about sixty," I grin.

"Sixty?" She winces.

"Can humans not hold their breath for sixty counts comfortably?" I understand not having gills, but having barely any breath control seems like overall poor design for humans as a species.

She holds out a hand and rocks it from side to side, in what I can only assume is an uncertain answer.

"I could swim faster?"

Her face is cautiously optimistic.

"I could still breathe for you, I promise it's not—"

Leeenuh holds her hand up to silence me, no words are needed to know that she'd like to try it on her own.

She doesn't seem too frightened of the prospect, though, as she makes a diving motion out of the cave's entrance.

"Oh no, you hold on to me and we'll go in together." I give sweet Leeenuh little warning before sweeping her off her feet, my arms wrapping around her torso. "Are you ready?"

When she nods, I take it as my cue to jump through the opening feetfirst, not wanting to risk hitting her head with a dive.

The initial rush of water is shocking, but I'm reassured when my Leeenuh is still clinging to me. Her cheeks are puffed large as I make my initial kicks toward the surface.

I work the muscles in my legs harder and harder, trying to cut down the fifty-five counts. I'm worried her human lungs might not handle that comfortably.

I push down the thought of this journey causing her harm as she tightens her hold. I can't pretend that I don't savor the feeling of her blunt little nails digging into the skin of my back.

I take a glance down at her face and notice her eyes are tightly shut.

We pass the dredlin, their scales shimmering with their rainbow of colors.

I feel Leeenuh shift on me slightly and when I look at her face, I'm nervous at how red it's become. Seeing her in distress must trigger some biological response in me because as I accelerate toward the surface, I can feel the adrenaline coursing through my veins, barely missing a dredlin's body in my haste.

Leeenuh emerges from beneath the water, gasping for breath. She clasps her hands at my back as she pants, dropping her forehead against my chest.

"Tat ha two hive bin longur dan a minit," Leeenuh chokes out.

"It's alright, you did great!" I say as one brother strokes her back.

She's so exhausted from the effort to simply get to the surface. Her breathing seems to slow a bit, and her body relaxes. She shifts her legs, hooking them more securely around my back, and settles her head into the crook of my neck.

My cock hardens against my will. What's wrong with me? A simple snuggle of her body and my cock is ready to burst.

Focus, Kitaico.

I tread water toward the rocky shoreline, trying to gauge which spot might have the best footholds to get Leeenuh ashore comfortably. I spy a smoother portion, likely refined by the waves over the eons. It will surely be a slippery ascent, but I think I'm less likely to hurt her on that specific portion of rock.

There's a steep section, about two of me tall, that we'll have to scale before cresting over the edge and onto dry land. Kitaico of the past would have just jumped up and hoped for the best.

But the days when I would scale the shore's overhang recklessly, letting my tentacles do most of the work, are gone. I can't be careless with my mate in my arms. I swim over, making sure her ankles are notched tightly behind my back, and use my arms and my foretentacles to grip and hoist our bodies into the spray crashing against the rocks.

"Hold on tightly, Leeenuh!" I yell.

My foot slips, and I stumble forward, nearly hitting the back of Leeenuh's head against the rock before one brother snakes around her skull protectively. She doesn't seem to notice the near miss and I thank the Great Mother I didn't drop her.

Once I'm steadier, the brothers snake upward, higher than my arms can reach. With a grunt, and no small amount of effort, I pull us both up over the jagged ledge.

When we arrive on solid ground, she moves her legs as though she might get down. I place a hand over her ass, stopping her attempt to dismount.

"Not yet, we've got longer to walk, and I would feel better if you let me carry you the rest of the way," I say nobly.

Her human skin always seems fragile to me, and I don't want to set her down on the lava rocks. I fear they might tear into her soft little feet.

She rolls her eyes but doesn't resist.

As I walk closer to the dense jungle forest, vines and leaves in all shades of pink, red, and orange wrap around us as we enter the brush. Leeenuh squints as she tries to take in her surroundings. The light dims as we enter the tree line.

Although revered by our Fi'len cousins, the Andjin have no ceremonial use for the hot springs. But that doesn't mean we don't enjoy the warm waters or their supposed healing properties.

I turn left at an ancient stone marker.

"We're almost there Leeenuh," I tell the top of her head.

When she looks up, her eyes go wide, and I wonder if she spots she the flying bukkau that reside here. Their muscular bodies and huge maws can be quite the intimidating sight. It sails though the trees, attempting to gather some of the nuite fruit. They're large and intimidating as they flap their leathery wings overhead.

"Don't worry Leeenuh, the bukkau don't find you nearly as tasty as I do." The words fall from my lips before I can stop myself.

As tasty as I do?

I have always known that I lack subtlety, but this is a new low.

The comment must not bother Leeenuh too much, though, because she chuckles.

Maybe she's not as put out at the thought of my tongue on her as I thought. My chest burns with the thought of dipping my tongue into her perfect cunt. She could get what she needs from me, and I would love nothing more than to taste her.

My cock swells beneath my wrap, and I flex my ass muscles, trying to get comfortable. I hate wearing anything outside of the capital, especially something as restrictive and itchy as a woven wrap.

I try to focus on something that isn't Leeenuh, her cunt, the delicious way she smells, or really anything about her at all. Since we're out of the safety of the nest, I would prefer to keep all the blood near my brain.

The hot springs, although not a popular Andjin destination, aren't a secret spot. Any Andjin could be there today, and maybe, if our luck is bad, we could run into an exiled male.

But given that the Great Proving is in full swing, they normally stick to the ocean.

I know I am more than capable of protecting Leeenuh from an exile; I am strong, in my prime, and will protect her with my life.

Maybe we're not so far off from true mates...I wouldn't die for a stranger, would I?

Leeenuh wrinkles her nose as we approach the water's edge. They smell interesting compared to the ocean, but nothing I find too offensive.

"I think they smell that way because they're medicinal. They do have an acquired aroma, though," I laugh as I set her down on the lip of the pool.

"Ould't bee urse dan an algae covurd layke, ight?" She chuckles her nonsense words.

"Leeenuh, you are delightful even if I don't understand what you're saying," I say as I slide into the warm waters.

I must be more on edge than I thought, because at the first touch of the heated liquid, my muscles relax. I didn't know I'd been holding my body so tightly. Has caring for her made me hold on to some unconscious stress?

I lean back, letting my head rest on the rocky edge, relaxing my body for, I suppose, the first time since Leeenuh's arrival.

I can't stop myself as I let my gaze trail up Leeenuh's curves when she removes her wrap skirt and damaged body suit. She's completely naked as she slowly slips into the pool.

I've seen her nude before, touched her naked body. I shouldn't be shy about the vision of perfection in front of me. But every time I see her little human form, warmth fills me, and I can't help it when a giddy smile cracks across my face.

She is truly stunning, in a way so alien I never thought it possible. I love every dip and curve of her soft body, especially her breasts. They are much more swollen than an Andjin female's.

My mouth salivates as I think of what it might be like to take her nipple between my lips. There is no hope of talking my erection down, so I do nothing to hide it. She shimmies over to me, the water making her breasts bob deliciously as she moves.

She settles against my side. Our thighs touch and I twitch, using all my willpower to stop myself from reaching out for her.

"I love the way you feel against me," I tell her sincerely.

I'm surprised though when she grabs my hand and pulls my arm over her shoulder.

I'm holding my breath as she mutters some of her human words into my skin. The brothers respond to her closeness and slide over her arms.

I ramble, unsure of where this is leading. "Does the water feel good, Leeenuh? I hope it feels better than the shower. That was the whole point of coming—"

My voice sticks in my throat as her hand touches my cock. I don't move a muscle as she glides her arched fingers down my hard length.

"Leeenuh," I moan, "what are you doing?"

helping hands

Lena

EVEN I'M a little surprised at how comfortable I feel being naked in front of Kitaico. I didn't think twice about stripping down before I hopped in. Sure, part of it was the fact that the clothes were soaked and cold, but another part of me just feels safe with him.

When I catch his eye, he's trying his hardest to make sure his gaze is fixed on my face. He's obviously attempting not to look at my tits, and my nipples ache, remembering his foretentacles on them earlier. His jaw is set, even as I can see his body relax a bit in the heat of the pool.

It's like we're in a little jungle grotto, and the way the pool's water glows an effervescent teal is like something out of a fairy tale.

The sparkling ethereal water is also incredibly translucent, which gives me a perfect view of Kitaico's alien cock.

A few days ago, I might have tried my best to keep my eyes up, too. The thought of having to acknowledge he was hard in front of me might have even been embarrassing. Now though? After I've felt his tentacles pulsating inside me, after him telling me he wants to taste me? It turns me on to see the effect I have on him.

And unlike my tainted blood, there's no crazy hormone inducing venom inspiring his feelings for me. Kitaico wants me right now, just as I am. He's been so fucking kind, and he literally saved my life. These feelings I'm developing for him can't just be the venom, can they?

As I slide to sit next to him, I grab his arm and wrap it around me. His eyes shine like I'm the entire world as he appraises me.

"Does the water feel good, Leeenuh?" God, even the way he mispronounces my name is endearing. "I hope it feels better than the shower. That was the whole point of coming—" Kitaico's voice sticks in his throat as I grab his hard cock.

My fingers don't touch around him as he's too big, but I do my best to slide my palm over all of him. I twist my fingers as I stroke down his throbbing shaft.

Pausing, I wait for him to tell me to keep going, or stop, or just anything. But Kitaico is frozen as his skin shifts to a bright blue that ebbs into purple.

"Leeenuh," his voice cracks, "are you starting your heat early?" He almost shakes with the concentration I assume being still is taking him.

"No." I shake my head. "You need help. Let me help you—like you've helped me?" I try to convey with gestures.

"I…should we do such things out in the open?" Kitaico is flustered, and it only emboldens me more.

"Yes." I keep my response short, giving his cock another stroke.

As I grip his skin, I can tell Kitaico is aquatic. His pre-cum under the water forms some kind of lubed barrier to the normal chafing an underwater hand job might cause.

"If this is what you truly want, I am yours." His voice deepens, pupils blowing wide as he relaxes into my touch.

Kitaico traces his large hand over my thigh, dipping his fingers lower, skirting my mound. I pull it away with my free hand.

"Just you." I point at him as I pay attention to the head of his weeping cock.

The short pubic tentacles around the base of his dick grasp desperately onto my hand.

"Oh, Leeenuh, this isn't necessary, I promise you—"

I cut him off with a kiss, my lips pressing hard against his mouth.

"Just shut up and let it happen," I chuckle, pulling away from him.

Kitaico's eyes are still closed as he brings a hand to his mouth, like he's savoring our touch.

He only opens them as I straddle him, attempting to give him the best view. It takes a while to steady my hips. Ultimately, I require Kitaico to anchor me from sliding away by pulling myself against him, his hand firmly clutching my ass.

I nestle tightly against him, aligning our bodies in a way that allows me to reach his erection. The position also lets him watch me as I work. To think I avoided looking at this beauty of a dick for so long.

Kitaico is thick with a graceful skyward arch. As my hand moves up and down, I feel the pronounced ridges running along his entire length. I think about how good he would feel inside me, like a real life "ribbed for her pleasure" scenario.

Suddenly, his dick's tentacles touch my aroused pussy lips, sending sparks down my spine. Their gentle tugs and teasing motions on my labia set me on fire. My muscles contract with anticipation. I moan as one appendage runs itself up my slick slit.

"I'm sorry, Leeenuh," the flushed alien grits out. "I can't control my mating crest, not when you're this close."

Mating crest, so it has a name.

"It's okay," I purr, cupping his cheek. "You're a good boy and you deserve a release."

I take the hand not stroking his cock and cradle his balls, tugging them softly away from his shaft. Kitaico bites his lip, stifling a moan.

"Don't be quiet," I command as I bring a hand up and force his mouth open into an O. His face flashes with surprise, but when I set back to work on his manhood, he recovers quickly.

"Leeenuh, this feels so good, so much better than I've imagined," he mewls as he tilts his head back, leaning it on the pool's edge. Kitaico's hips thrust upward, his skin rippling with different colors as he does.

I can feel his sac tightening, and I'm nearly lifted out of the water with how high he's thrusting. He holds onto me during this wild ride, his fingers digging deep into the meat of my ass.

"Be still," I tell him, placing a hand on his pec, conveying my instructions.

He nods shakily as I pick up my pace, the slickness of his dick making it easy. I hum to myself as I get a good rhythm down. At his head, I apply more pressure, milking his cock. Meanwhile, at the base, I grip the root of him tightly, holding the blood inside his stiff member.

His hips jerk up frantically again, his eyes rolling back. I can feel his muscles contracting, signaling his impending release. In response, leaning forward, I press my hips against his body, creating a delicious friction.

I pull him closer, wrapping my hand around the nape of his neck, and kiss him greedily. Our tongues search each other's mouths as I slide my dripping pussy up and down his massive shaft. The ribs of his cock hit my clit with damn near every movement.

He brings a hand up to my face and as he comes, I can feel his fang bite into my lip. It hurts, but I'm too distracted by the coiling of my core. Kitaico's cum floats up from the water between us as I keep rocking against him. When our mouths break, I'm panting and his tongue swipes the blood from my lip.

"I am sorry to have hurt you, you're so perfect." Kitaico sighs as his lips touch my forehead. He smooths my hair back, still peppering me with frantic kisses. "You make me feel so good."

"Will you come for me Leeenuh? Do you want to ride my throbbing cock to bliss?"

His breath fans over my neck as he licks my pulse point. I keep grinding against him selfishly, searching for my own release.

"If you would let me, I'd drive my cock deep into your slick cunt. I'd never let you go." He moans into my ear. "I would do anything to keep you, mate."

He's rambling, lost in some post orgasm haze—but his words have me going feral. I want Kitaico—and I want Kitaico to want me.

"You're more than I could have ever dreamed of. I'm not worthy," he groans as I shatter over him. My body jolts, and I let the waves of stars wash over me.

Strong arms wrap around me, and my whole body vibrates with satisfaction. His giant hand tucks my head against his chest as we sink deeper into the warm waters.

"Thank you," he whispers as I lie boneless on his chest.

Maybe the universe isn't indifferent, maybe every step was leading me here, to him.

Suddenly there's a crunching behind us, some snapping of twigs and shuffling of leaves. Kitaico tenses and stands, wrapping my legs tightly around his back.

"What is it? Another one of those dinosaur birds?" I ask my protector.

"We have to go, Leeenuh," he says with urgency, pulling us out of the pool and swiftly retracing our steps back to the shore.

"Kitaico," I gasp, my body still trembling with the aftermath of my climax. He ignores me until I thump him on the chest.

"Kitaico!" I whisper, "What's wrong?"

His feet move even faster, his heart thudding loudly in his chest.

"Exiles. We must return to the safety of the nest. Stay silent and hold on to me tightly," he says with a grave expression.

blaster barbeque

EXILES.

The word seems to slow down time. I know Kitaico is sprinting to the seashore, my body bouncing violently as he does —but everything feels like we're moving through molasses, like we can't run quickly enough.

It feels like we'll get fucking caught.

My senses, which just seconds ago were blurred with a post orgasm glow, twist and distort as fear floods my system.

"Leeenuh, we're nearing the shore. I need you to hold your breath!" Kitaico mutters. His feet showing no signs of stopping their pounding through the field of lava stone.

"Okay." I breathe deeply, readying my lungs.

There's a noise behind Kitaico's back. Something big sounds like it's scrambling as it slips on the jagged rocks of the shoreline.

I press the tip of my nose over Kitaico's shoulder, trying to get a better glimpse of who is chasing us right as his feet leave the cliff. He arches his body, gripping me tightly, and dives into the water.

For the briefest of moments, I see the snarling vision of horror that trails closely.

Fangs lengthen as he stretches out a hand tipped with jagged claws. Its tentacles flare wildly around its scarred visage. His pupils are pinpricks and his face conveys nothing but a manic need. The alien is the same as Kitaico, an Andjin, but that's where the similarities stop.

Exiles want nothing more than a mate. Kitaico's words flood my mind as I face this nightmare creature behind me.

He wants me.

The exiled male's skin, a vibrant shade of crimson, catches my eye before I gulp and hold my breath.

The pursuing creature is getting dangerously close, and I can smell the exiles' breath just before my head submerges in the cool saltwater.

Kitaico's legs kick as relentless as a machine. With each stroke, his thighs exhibit taut and powerful muscles.

I refuse to open my eyes again, afraid of seeing the monster pursuing us.

Tightening my grasp on Kitaico, I realize the incredible stroke of luck I must have had. Luck that brought this gentle male to my side, instead of that crazed thing chasing us now. If that creature had been the one to discover me, would I have survived?

I suppress the thought, trying to control my panic levels. The burning in my chest won't subside if I keep imagining the worst possible outcomes. Instead, I press my ear against Kitaico's chest and listen to the rhythmic thump of his heart.

He'll protect me, he promised.

My chest tightens, fighting against the suffocating sensation of airlessness. The spasms ripple through my torso, causing waves of pain to radiate outward.

"Almost there, hold on!" Kitaico yelps, but the sound is warped and twisted by the water surrounding us.

Suddenly, his feet kick off an object, causing us both to pivot quickly back up. With Kitaico's forceful push, I'm thrown into the nest, feeling like a rag doll. When my head finally emerges from the water, I gasp for air, and the sound echoes in the silence.

My fingernails claw up on the ledge of the opening before I pull myself onto the cave floor. Adrenaline still teems through my veins. Finally, with one last surge of strength, I pull myself up and onto the cave floor, my body thudding against the ground. Water drips off my naked skin as I shake on the floor. I can't tell if it's the cold or the dread I feel as I turn my head and look at the entrance to the nest.

Time stills as I wait for Kitaico to pop up behind me—but he doesn't.

The water churns and splashes. There's a ruckus occurring beneath its surface.

I can't just lie here. What if Kitaico needs my help?

I push myself up, searching the cave for something to protect myself with. Rope, dried fish, nuite fruit, everything here is so unlethal! I slam my fist against the store shelves in frustration.

That's when I hear it, the faint clang of metal on metal resonating from the top shelf. Too short to identify the source of the mysterious sound, I decide to climb up. I slip only once, but the rock skins the palm of my hand, and I bite my lip to push down the pain.

After much effort, I finally reach the top shelf and discover the origin of the noises—shining, deadly, and entirely out of place is a blaster gun.

I'm shocked that something as high tech as this even exists in this primitive setting. I've never shot one, but I've seen blasters used before. It shouldn't be harder to figure out than a human gun, should it?

I put the weapon in my hands, and turn it to either side, frantically looking for the safety. When I think I find it, I hold the barrel away from me, clicking the button forward with my eyes closed. It's like I'm afraid that I'll accidentally hit a self-destruct button instead.

But it doesn't blow up, and I can feel it shake as the power surges through the pistol. I clench it in my hands as I jump off the shelf, aiming it toward the opening.

The water still churns and gurgles, and I swear I hear a muffled scream—I can't tell if it's Kitaico or not.

The water changes colors. An inky blackness spins up and spreads until the darkness engulfs the entire opening.

Sweat drips from my wet brow, my heart in my throat, as I'm forced to wait for someone or something to come through that hole.

Finally, with a wet thump, a red and scarred foretentacle slides up through the water.

Kitaico didn't win.

I push down the grief welling in my chest and let the rage that's left take hold. With a strange precision, I point the blaster. My hand will be ready to pull the trigger as soon as I see the bastard's eyes.

Keep breathing, in and out. Don't fuck this up, Lena, you might only get one shot.

It feels like hours, but must only be seconds, as a head surfaces.

It's only after I've half depressed the trigger do I realize that it's Kitaico's face looking back at me. Just before the plasma blast leaves the gun, I rip it to the side, hoping with every part of my being that I'll miss.

Everything is slowing down again. Each beat of my heart takes minutes.

The realization that I'm shooting at him spreads over his face. Kitaico's eyes go wide, and he dives to the side. His tentacles flail through the air as he moves, like a lion's mane in motion. I snap my eyes closed again, letting the blaster drop to the ground with a clank.

I hear the sizzle of flesh when the plasma beam connects with his skin. There's the scent of barbeque and an alien sounding expletive that leaves Kitaico's lips.

I've fucking shot my alien lover.

keep her or die trying

WHEN I UNCOVER my hands from my head, the exiled male's detached foretentacle is still wriggling in my grip.

Blinking slowly, I turn to Leeenuh. Her eyes are shut tightly even though she's crying. Fat wet tears slide down her cheeks.

"Arr ewe ded? Did eye urt chew, Kitaico?" she sobs.

I pat my chest with my free hand and find no hole left by the blaster gun.

With a sharp inhale, the scent of burning flesh reaches my nose, causing a wave of nausea to wash over me. Only while combing my hand through my tentacles do I find the injury.

Leeenuh has blown one tip of my lesser head tentacles clean off. The blaster's cauterizing function prevented any bleeding from the wound.

I'm okay.

Hopping through the cave's entrance, a wave of relief washes over me. Leeenuh is alright, that's all the matters. I quickly rush over to my distraught mate, needing to comfort her. Witnessing her in such distress is like getting punched in the gut.

"Leeenuh," I say, stroking her cheek, "I am fine."

She peeks open one of her eyes and looks at me.

Panic washes over her features as the other shoots open and she runs a hand over my face, pulling it back and holding it up for me to see the blackness that covers it.

"It is only blood," I mutter.

She inhales sharply, eyes going even wider.

"Not mine," I correct, holding the exile's tentacle. You can still make out my fang marks from when I bit it off his body.

She doesn't calm down much but rushes to grab one of our woven rags from the store shelves. Leeenuh wipes the offending fluid from my face and arms.

"Eye'm so so soarry," she keeps saying repeatedly. "Eye shouldn't ave dun dat thur. Eye forgot auhbout da exiles."

I grasp her wrist, stopping her motions. Her arm trembles uncontrollably in my grip.

Taking the soiled cloth from her, I step under the cool spray of the shower, washing away the rest of the blood.

"This isn't your fault," I say, feeling so stupid for leaving the safety of the nest. With a grimace, I fling the exile's tentacle down the relief hole, hoping it will decompose along with the rest of our waste.

Before I can even step out of the shower, Leeenuh rushes toward me, embracing me. She buries her face in my chest, and I instinctively shield her from the water. I hold her against me, feeling powerless as she continues to cry.

Hoping to comfort her, I press my lips to the top of her head in a human gesture.

It must work, because I feel her shoulders shake a little less by the time I'm gathering her up in my arms. Her naked body is shivering, though, and I lay her in the nest before wrapping her tightly in every blanket I have.

I kick myself for not grabbing her clothing but remember that there's no way that flimsy and torn piece of material could keep my human warm.

I curl up next to her, letting the heat of my body help her current predicament.

There's just something about Leeenuh that feels like home. It's the way she fits against me, like her strange small proportions were made to sleeve against mine.

"How'd you know about the blaster?" I ask, my curiosity piquing when I feel the burned off tentacle rub against the blanket.

Leeenuh points to her eyes with two fingers, then to the top shelf where it was stored.

"You looked? How observant of you," I chuckle, gripping her tighter.

"Weye du ewe hav dat?" she asks something, pointing at the blaster on the floor.

"Do you want to know why there's a blaster in the nest?"

She nods.

"It's for," I pause, unsure of how much I should tell her. Will this help our current situation any or just make her feel worse?

She turns back, staring into my soul as she waits for an answer.

I can't lie to her, and I never will.

She's my mate, she deserves the truth.

"If I'm unable to complete the first portion of the Great Proving for any reason…injury, isolation, insanity, or cowardice. The blaster is for that. It is better not to come home than to come home a failure." I tell her solemnly. "The elders give each potential male one before we leave the capital."

Her face drops as she realizes the blaster's intended purpose.

She points over to it again. "Wats dat liyet?"

I turn my attention to the weapon on the floor. A soft white light blinks near the trigger.

The homing beacon.

"The elders…they're coming to collect my body. They assumed I have failed this portion of my Great Proving."

As the adrenaline from the fight leaves my system, I jolt up with the realization of what's about to happen. The blasters are monitored by the elders. They can be remotely deactivated if a Great Proving candidate goes rogue. The elders are coming, and I'm going to have to explain what's been going on with Leeenuh here in my nest.

I'll have to explain her mating mark…

I gaze at her small naked body.

"We have to get you dressed." There's a frantic edge to my voice. The thought of another male looking at her in this state has my blood boiling.

Even the elders, the leaders of our people, don't get to look at her like this.

Despite having no mating mark of my own, I know she's mine. I'll have to prove I am worthy of her to the elders.

I will keep her or die trying.

a sniff too far

KITAICO IS frantic with the expected arrival of the mysterious elders. He's even got me wrapped tightly in a bedsheet, toga style, which is as modest as I've ever been in space.

Grabbing another strip of woven cloth, he wraps my hand, covering my mating mark.

"Why are you doing that?" I ask, the worry that he's somehow embarrassed of me filling me with dread. Does he not want his people to see he's mated an alien?

He just keeps fussing with the knot until I place my hand on top of his.

Kitaico tilts his face to mine, and although we can't understand each other, I must wear my emotions plain as day on my face.

"Oh, oh no," he whispers, cradling my face in his hands, his eyes brimming with concern. "I could never be ashamed of you. There are just specifics that need to be discussed before we should reveal what has happened between us. I'm afraid they'll find me undeserving of a mate as wonderful as you." Kitaico's voice is soft as he presses a kiss to my forehead. "I will scream my devotion to you from the mountaintops, but only once I know it's safe for us both."

I know he's right, but it still feels so wrong to have the mark covered. I don't understand his world, or his customs, so I need to let him take the lead on this.

"The exile?" I change the subject, pointing toward the cave's opening. "Is he dead?" My finger slides across my throat in a slicing motion.

"We don't need to worry about the exile. I'm sure my venom pumping through his veins has dispatched him by now." He grimaces, running his tongue over his lips. Does he remember the taste of his blood?

"Your venom?" Surely, he didn't pump the exile full of mating chemicals?

"Oh, a different venom all together, much more lethal." He flashes me his fangs and runs the tip of his tongue across their points.

"Glad to hear I won't have any competition in the horny for Kitaico category." I breathe a sigh of relief, then touch the small scab on my lip, remembering his fang. "But wait—"

"Oh no, no, no." His eyes go wide. "I have to engage my venom, and I would never do that to you!" He places his hands over my arms reassuringly.

"Okay, good," I say, letting out a breath.

"Just let me do the talking, Leeenuh, I promise everything will turn out okay." He sits down on the bed, patting the area beside him for me to follow. He taps his foot and fingers the burned tentacle.

I still can't believe I shot him. The guilt has me leaning hard against him, searching for comfort.

"It'll be fine. I'll explain everything and they'll have no choice but to let us stay together. You're my mate, after all." He's rambling, as if he's trying to convince himself as much as he is me.

I slide my fabric covered palm onto his thigh, and he stops talking. His big square hand grips my own, and he gulps nervously. We sit there in silence, waiting for what will hopefully be a happy fate.

With my eyes fixed on the entrance to the cave, I can't miss the lights and bubbles that eventually come. I'm not sure how long I thought it would take the elders to arrive, but it feels like it's taken too long and yet somehow not long enough when they finally do.

The first to enter is an armed guard, built much like Kitaico, but scarred and stern looking. He sees the blaster discarded on the floor first, before clocking us holding hands. His brows screw up as he looks at me.

Maybe I'm the first human he's ever seen?

The next two Andjin to surface are older and dressed in miraculously dry beaded robes. The fabric repels the water quickly, and it puddles at their feet.

The color of both their skins is much more muted than the younger Andjin in the room. I wonder if losing their color could be like when a human's hair goes gray.

They seem less confused than the guard, and more incredibly displeased.

"Kitaico, we're here because your blaster was discharged— we expected to claim your body to return to your parents," one elder says.

The other finishes, disgusted with the situation at hand. "But it seems there are other circumstances afoot. What is this female doing in your nest? You are not yet found worthy of mating— you know this offense is punishable by death! Where did this strange creature come from?"

The situation being me, I guess.

"This female, Leeenuh, fell from the sky. If not for my rescue, she would have succumbed to the scripiat," he says as he bows his head. I assume it's a sign of respect, so I do the same.

"So you kept her here? Instead of informing the council of

elders? What if she's a spy sent by the Fi'len army?" one elder yells.

If I wasn't so worried about the offhanded comment about Kitaico being put to death, I might laugh at the absurdity of the spy comment.

I am the least sneaky person alive.

"She is not. I stake my life on it," he says, head still lowered.

The elder who has yelled less, raises a hand right as the one scolding us opens his mouth.

"Enough Gunkoi, Surely, there is a reasonable explanation for what has occurred in this mating hopeful's nest."

The angry one sets his jaw but stays silent. It's obvious from their interaction that Gunkoi isn't the one in charge.

I file that information away for later, just like the little details I used to remember whenever we arrived at a new station as a bubble babe.

I feel like some kind of circus animal that they're just leering at.

"Female," he continues, pointing at me.

I swallow down the fear in my throat and look him dead in the eyes.

"Has hopeful Kitaico harmed you or forced you into his mating bed?"

"Kitaico?" This time I do laugh. My alien turns to me, his face serious. "Of course not. He's been kinder than anyone I've ever met."

I turn to him and squeeze his hand. His skin ripples in shades of gray. His face is still drawn with worry, and I realize he doesn't understand me.

"No, he would never hurt me," I repeat, smiling at my mate.

"I am glad for it," the elder in charge says coolly. "Regardless, there are questions that must still be answered. Why didn't you bring her to the capital?"

"I did not wish to disqualify myself by leaving the nest. I

assessed the situation, and as Leeenuh was unharmed, I decided to bring her when I returned for the final challenge."

Both elders look at each other with some unspoken criticism of his answer. It must be an adequate response, as they don't pry further.

"Might I ask why the blaster was discharged?" Gunkoi asks, his brows knitting.

"That was my fault!" I offer. Kitaico squeezes my hand back with a drawn mouth. I think he's willing me to shut up, but I've already begun explaining. "An exile was trying to kidnap me, and I wasn't sure who would come through the entrance. I didn't realize it was Kitaico until I'd already shot. Luckily, I'm terrible with firearms, so I missed—mostly."

All the Andjin grimace as I point to his burnt tentacle.

"And what became of the exile?"

"Dead," Kitaico says plainly.

"Ah, I see," the elder says, scanning the cave thoughtfully. "As much as I hate being in another male's nest, I commend you for the work you've done, Kitaico. I'd like to continue our conversation back at the capital. You have much to prepare for. We'll allow you to continue your Great Proving journey."

"Thank you, Chancellor Hirouz. May the Great Mother allow me to bring honor to our people," Kitaico mutters, doing several quick motions with his fingers before thumping his fist on his chest.

Was that some kind of alien secret handshake?

"The female can travel?" Chancellor Hirouz asks.

"She has no gills." Kitaico points out my evolutionary short-comings.

"Ah, well, I will arrange for an additional pod," the elder says before tapping a techy-looking broach on his jacket. He mutters into the device, "Transport requested at the nesting site."

I turn my attention back to the scarred guard, who eyes me with curiosity. His face is almost as intrigued as it is distrusting, like he's trying to figure me out.

He scooped up the blaster from the floor while we weren't paying attention and holstered it at his hip.

I'm surprised at how high-tech the rest of the weapons strapped to the guard are. This planet seemed so primitive before.

But then again, I've been stuck in a cave, horny for Kitaico for most of it...

The guard takes a step closer and sniffs. Any confusion about me slips from his face.

"Chancellor Hirouz, I think the hopeful has been breeding with the female." His voice is grave.

"Hey, my name is Lena, and I have done nothing I didn't want to!" I don't like this guard's vibe, so I give him my best scowl.

Kitaico's eyes go wide as he watches the elders step closer and draw in the same awkward sniff as the guard.

"It would appear as though we still have much to discuss, Kitaico. Officer Rionkuj, please restrain the hopeful."

"I can't understand what she's saying"—he taps his temple—"but I promise you there's an explanation for whatever she's said."

"I expect there is. Please activate his translator chip as well. I wouldn't want the female to have to repeat herself." Chancellor Hirouz waves as the guard clamps both Kitaico's hands and foretentacles behind his head.

Even though Kitaico's face is forlorn, the brothers struggle in their restraints. They reach toward me as he's led to the entrance. The guard pushes a small key fob device up against his temple and my alien winces.

"Are you okay, Kitaico?" I ask, panicking as I see the only person I know on this planet cuffed.

Despite our circumstances, he turns to me and smiles.

"Your voice is even more beautiful when I can understand what you're saying."

the jewels

"JUST A FEW SECONDS of swimming and we'll be in the pod. Don't worry!" I tell my scared human mate.

She nods, drawing a deep breath into her lungs. The guard reaches out to assist her down into the water, but I bare my fangs at him with a hiss.

"Watch yourself," he says. "I'm only assisting the female, so we might avoid injuries. I have no desire to touch her beyond that."

The officer holds his hand up, revealing the same purple mating mark that Leeenuh is hiding.

"Be gentle with her. Restraints or not, I will kill you if you hurt her," I say boldly.

"Understood," he says, unsurprised at my protectiveness.

"Hey, I'll be okay, Kitaico. Take some deep breaths. I can handle myself." Leeenuh tries to reassure me.

So I do my best to stuff down the urge to bite out the guard's throat. He has a mate, and Leeenuh isn't scared.

We have bigger things to worry about right now, anyway.

I jump into the sea and make my way to the airlock of the secondary pod. The elders have already returned to their vehicle.

When I turn, kicking my legs to pivot in the water, I see Leeenuh. She's being held by the guard at arm's length, as he's trying desperately not to touch her any more than necessary. Her eyes are shut tight, and her cheeks are puffed large with air.

Once they've both made it all the way into the airlock, the guard depresses a button on the control panel. The hatch door clicks shut and saltwater rushes out of the chamber as the air is forced in. Leeenuh stumbles forward, adjusting to the pressure, and falls into my chest. I steady her, wishing my arms were free. But as she rights herself, I kiss her forehead, earning a stern look from the guard.

"Refrain from touching the female, hopeful," he barks as he opens the second hatch into the seating area of the pod.

He guides Leeenuh to a chair before shoving me into one facing hers.

The guard, blessedly, sits as far on the other side of the small cabin as he can.

"Kitaico," Leeenuh whispers, drawing my attention back to her, "is everything still going to be okay? I mean, I guess we don't need to worry about the exile now... but seeing you in cuffs has me worried."

She furrows her brow as I shift uncomfortably in my seat. My arms are behind my back, the position not allowing me to sit naturally.

"Trust me and try to let me handle things from now on." I know it has to be hard for her to contain her conversation. She's not been understood for so long.

"I...I'm just being honest. I don't think honesty can hurt us in this situation, can it? Are you mad at me?" she asks softly.

"No, sweet Leeenuh, you deserve to speak the truth...I just don't want to be separated from you. We need to explain—" I look at the guard, who's now engrossed in something on his datapad, and lower my voice. "Your mark."

"I mean, it happened. It was an accident, but I'm not upset that it did. My experiences with other species in space haven't been good." She rubs the mark through the makeshift bandage. My blood pressure spikes, thinking of anyone being cruel to the female across from me. How anyone could fathom doing anything but cherishing her is a mystery to me.

She is divine.

"But you, you are the exception. At first, I wasn't sure if I could see myself"—she mouths the word mated before continuing—"to an alien stranger…but I know you now. I know that you'll care for me no matter what and that your lack of a mark means nothing. We belong together. I fought it at first, thinking it was a, er, chemical response. But it's deeper than that, Kitaico. I think this thing between us could work." Her eyes are wet as she talks.

"Do you mean it, Leeenuh?" Hope wells in my chest. Could someone as wonderful as Leeenuh be who I've been fated for?

"It's Lena," she says with a chuckle.

Lena.

I've been saying her name wrong this whole time?

"I'm so sorry. I didn't mean to bring dishonor to your name by pronouncing it wrong. Forgive me!" I drop my chin to my chest, embarrassed. How could I have not noticed?

She leans forward, using her index finger to tilt my jaw back up to hers.

"I like my name, anyway you say it. We're in this together, right?"

"Always."

I close my eyes as she presses her lips to mine. The heat of her body lets me momentarily forget myself. I moan into her mouth, searching it with my tongue.

Lena pulls away, and I hear a heavy foot thump on the floor.

"Enough, you disgrace the Proving, hopeful. Sleep now, before you shame your family name any further."

My eyes shoot open just in time to see the guard coming my way, tranquilizer gun in hand.

The guard pushes me back down into my seat.

"Stay put, female, he's fine," he says gruffly.

"Fine? He's fucking unconscious!" I yell back at him.

How in the hell am I supposed to let Kitaico handle all the talking while he's slumped forward in his seat?

This whole situation is fucked, but I've never let anyone push me around on Earth and I won't start now.

"Hey, noodle head!" I yell at the guard, who was returning to his seat.

He stops dead in his tracks. A sigh escapes his alien lips before he turns around. "Female, sit down and—"

I cut him off, throwing a pillow from the chair at his head. The soft square hits him right between the eyes with a dull thud. With yet another sigh, the guard turns and aims the tranquilizer gun he used on Kitaico straight at me.

"What the actual fuck, are you going to shoot—"

When I wake, I'm in what looks like a space-age prison cell. The bars are made of some orange laser light. I have a feeling that if I touch them, I'd get burned. I'm sitting on a cot and slumped against the wall. My shoulder stings when I rouse.

"Are you okay?" Kitaico's worried voice asks.

"Kitaico?" I scan the room, looking for my mate.

He's not too many cells down. He's sitting on his knees, looking directly at me when I find him.

"What are they going to do with us?" I ask, knowing that I probably should have kept my cool better than I did in the pod.

"I assume they'll want to question you, confirm you're not a spy…and then question me about, well, us," he mumbles.

"Will they try to separate us?"

"No, not once they understand what we are…what you are. They'll never dare to separate us once I've proven that I am worthy of a mate." He smiles reassuringly.

"You don't need to prove anything to anyone. I know you're going to be an amazing mate." I smile, wishing I could touch him.

"I am proud you see me as such"—his grin is sadder than my own—"but there is one last test to the Great Proving. I must defeat another hopeful in combat—to prove that I can properly protect a female."

"And you already did! You saved us both from that exile. I mean, you barely knew me, and you saved me from the whale monster when I arrived here." I try to talk some sense into him. There's nothing left to prove to me.

"Ah, the scripiat…" he mutters. "Unfortunately, it's important in my culture that I prove it to the others as well. Knowing you're here for me when I return will make my victory all the sweeter." He looks at me like I'm made of stardust.

"Kitaico, let's just tell them about the mark—they'll have to understand." I don't want to keep it a secret anymore. I want to show the elders. We can convince them we belong together. It is essential, despite what his culture says.

"No, we do this the right way—with honor. You are worth any hardship…Lena. This is a small thing to you, but an important one to me."

"Okay," I gulp down my anxiety, forcing myself to trust that Kitaico understands his culture more than I do.

Suddenly there's a whirring noise as a door panel slides open. A large group of ornately dressed elders enters the narrow hallway between the cells.

Chancellor Hirouz is at the head of the pack.

"So, we meet again, Lena." The way he says my name has me wanting to recoil from him.

"Kitaico was awake earlier and telling us about how you miraculously came to be in his care. Fallen from the sky like the Great Mother?" His tone shows that he doesn't believe a word Kitaico said. I don't know how my alien thinks I came to be on his planet. We never got the chance to talk about it.

"More like unceremoniously dumped from a Deenz transport unit," I scoff.

"The same Deenz the fi'len scum have waged war with?" he asks, like I have any bearing on current events.

"No idea! The fi'len were always nice though. Certainly nicer than our slavers," I say.

"You are a human from Earth, yes?"

The sound of my home planet's name makes my chest well with longing.

"Yes," I breathe.

I feel terrible that my gut instinct is to ask if they could take me home…back to my grandmother. But I don't want to leave Kitaico, and I know that he'll never be welcome on my planet.

"The fi'len queen is a human, and her king has made it his mission to destroy the Deenz entity—making war for us all," the chancellor says saltily.

"Sorry that my kidnapping has inconvenienced you," I snap, then realize they could just as easily put me back in the scaley purple hands that I was before. "Are you going to return me to the Deenz like some kind of lost property?"

"No, we would never harm a female, regardless of how strange you humans appear. From the information we've gained from Kitaico and our planetary security—you are not a state threat."

"Great, so let us out of here," I plead with the group of austere dignitaries.

"Patience, we are here to do just that."

With a click of the fancy broach, the orange laser bars of my cell buzz into nothingness. I step into the hall and wait patiently for Kitaico's own bars to drop. But they remain in place, light burning bright as ever.

My mate's camouflage shifts quickly, a sign of his nervousness, I've learned.

"And Kitaico?"

"Still needs to discuss some matters with the council. Do not fret, no harm will come to either of you as long as you comply." The chancellor glares at me, as if expecting me to act out.

"It's alright Lena, we'll meet up shortly, okay?" My mate gives me his most earnest face.

"Okay." I wrap my arms around myself. I'm in awe at how quickly we've come to rely on each other.

A guard arrives and is told to escort me to the jewels.

The jewels?

Despite my curiosity, I keep my mouth shut. My outbursts so far haven't helped.

I trace the swirling lines I know are under my bandages. The guard, a different one than from before, must pick up on my apprehension.

"You have nothing to be worried about, human. To be a female on the Korlyan Moon is to be treasured. So few of them remain." His words are kind, but he keeps his eyes straight ahead and his voice neutral. Maybe he's just trying to remain professional?

"Thanks," I whisper.

I look back over my shoulder at my mate before we walk down the unassuming corridor for what feels like miles.

Will they keep their word? Will I see Kitaico again?

I stare at my feet as I listen to the rhythm of our steps on the shiny stone floors. Abruptly, we stop, my nose nearly smashing into the guard's back as we do.

"What is your purpose here?" a stern voice says in front of us.

When I peek my head around my escort's torso, I see two more guards standing post beside a large door.

"To deliver this female to the care of the jewels," he says before stepping aside, leaving me awkwardly gawking as the two tentacled men appraise me.

"Female?" one says reverently.

"Yeah." I nod slowly.

"Compatible?" My head pivots as the other guard speaks.

"Um…" I'm not sure how to answer that question.

"Undetermined," my escort thankfully answers for me. "The Chancellor's orders are that she be remitted to the jewels."

The two guards nod, stepping aside. They both turn and press some kind of key fob into the wall panels on either side of the door. There's a clicking motion, and it slides open.

The aroma is the first thing that hits me. Sweet fruity notes and toasted incense. This place is such a contrast to the nest I've spent all my time in.

The view is just as opulent. This place must be as expensive as it smells. In the room, there's a set of circled chaise lounges. Maybe fifteen, each tufted with fine fabrics in jewel tones.

And on each of those sits what I can only assume are the Jewels.

Female Andjin of all shapes and colors recline. Soft alien bodies are dripping with precious stones and gold chains. Curled between delicate head tentacles are thin gold rings. I assume their level of modesty must be akin to that of my cloth-ing-hating mate when I see their bare chests. Everyone's nipples are adorned with what look like rings.

If I ever make it back to Earth, I'm going to have to tell Rachel, my tattoo shop's piercer, that aliens think nipple rings are just as hot as we do.

I realize I must be lost in awe as the guard nudges me with his knee to enter the room.

"Who is that?" one of the made-up females asks, her eyes dragging down my body judgmentally.

"Human female from Earth." The guard pauses and looks at me.

"Hi, I'm Lena."

picked apart

THE STARES ARE the only thing that cut through the silence as the guard sneaks out the door behind me. The feeling of being sized up and appraised as less than is universal, I realize as I'm silently picked apart.

"Lena." My name lingers on the lips of a pale chartreuse Andjin female who gracefully rises from her chaise and glides toward me.

My throat tightens, and I quickly gulp. Her commanding presence leaves no doubt that she will be the one to speak up on behalf of the group.

As she puts a hand on her hip, the stack of bangles on her wrist jingles softly.

"Are we supposed to usher you in? Are you to be fought for like the rest of us?" Her voice thankfully seems more annoyed than disgusted.

"To be honest, I don't know —" I pause for her name.

As if giving up, she sighs and says, "Yiskku. Come on, let's clean you up." She motions at the other women and as if they're her ladies-in-waiting, everyone follows her command.

Guided by several hands, I am pulled deeper into the jewels' den. With my arms raised in the air, I frantically attempt to maneuver out of the way, but their movements only grow stronger.

"She is a strange looking female," I hear a voice whisper behind me.

Wow, okay, weird thing for the tentacle alien to say, but sure. Despite not feeling like the weird one in the room, I subconsciously cover my midsection with my forearm, clutching my fingers into my rough homemade clothing.

"Oh shush Lyonui, just because she's different doesn't make her any less of a blessing from the goddess," Yiskku snaps. "And besides, she'll probably look ten thousand times better after a bath. She must be compatible if they've sent her up here. She deserves as much respect as the rest of you."

Her annoyed tone continues, but it's kind of nice that she's sticking up for me. I take note that she said you, and not us. Something tells me Yissku thinks herself the cream of the crop.

"Excuse me, can we talk about what you mean by compatible?" I ask, narrowing my eyes.

She turns her head, her brows raised.

"For breeding, obviously," she says with a smirk.

"Oh okay, sure." I can't help it when Kitaico's face flashes in my mind. "So, we can choose our mate, right?"

Kitaico is the only thing I have anymore, that kind, cinnamon roll of an alien. He saved me.

As the entire group chuckles at my question, a sinking feeling settles in my stomach.

"You, just like everyone here, will be a reward for the final challenge of the Great Proving."

They walk me into another chamber, this one filled with steam.

"But I'm not a reward, and there's already someone I—hey, I

can get that," I mutter. A pair of sky-blue hands are attempting to take off my toga.

"You can't bathe in those rags, you'll get the tub filthy," someone whines.

"But why even have this Great Proving? Surely you can choose your own mate, you seem like capable ladies!" I plaster a forced smile onto my lips.

I wiggle out of one grasping hand, only to fall into the grips of another. These "jewels" are a force to be reckoned with. If anyone should be scared, it should be the men of this world.

For a moment, the hands are still, and Yissku's voice cuts through the throng.

"It's a kindness. There are so few females left that to be a prize is safest. We deserve to be with the male most worthy of protecting us." Several tentacled heads nod, accepting their fates, before attempting to disrobe me once again.

"I've got it, really," I try to tell the throng of handsy women.

The nearness of the flock of females, the suffocating feeling of the steam, and the realization that I might never see Kitaico again come to a head. The panic truly sets in as they attempt to unravel the wrapping around my palm.

"Back the fuck up," I snap, pulling my hand against my chest.

"Excuse me?" Yiskku barks, her demeanor changing entirely.

"I'm not a prize," I say coldly. My fingers stumble, itching to unwrap my hand.

I don't know how I'm going to get my point across without showing them, though.

"I don't need any of this, because I already belong to someone."

"No one has been found worthy of you yet, but they will. It is a blessing, truly."

I pull the last bit of wrapping off my marked palm and ball it into a fist.

"I'm already someone else's *blessing*." Taking a deep breath, I show the group my mating mark.

It's like watching a train crash. The Andjin women flash a myriad of colors as the confusion sets in.

"Kitaico is mine, and I am his."

"Hopeful Kitaico has taken you as his mate…without being found worthy?" Yiskku's eyes go wide with horror.

"No, it was an accident. It was my fault." I shoulder the guilt for the mating sting, even though I don't really think there's any blame to assign.

It just happened.

"He'll be put to death," a voice in the crowd whispers.

"No, they've just taken him to talk to him…it's going to be okay—" I'm rambling, my eyes searching their now forlorn faces.

"He took a mate, without permission…" Yissku mutters.

"We consummated nothing." I blurt out, trying anything to convince them he deserves to live.

That statement gets their attention, and Yissku's brows raise.

"Even through your heats, he never touched you?" She doesn't believe me.

To be fair, I said mated, not touched.

"We never mated, I swear it." I hope that mating means a literal attempt at procreation. I will leave off the several instances of getting each other off if it means it'll save his life. Mating and touching aren't the same.

"No male could resist the urge to rut after taking his mate's mating sting, though. You lie!" A particularly judgy looking Andjin seethes.

"I don't have a stinger, or whatever you all do. I never marked him!" I hold up my wrist frantically to what feels like my jury.

Yissku grabs my arm and jabs a finger into the flesh where my stinger should be.

"She tells the truth. The alien has no mating barb." She

narrows her eyes. "But what of your heat? You took his venom, did you not?"

"He tied me up, restrained me so I wouldn't hurt myself or force myself on him. He kept telling me he hadn't been found worthy yet, that—"

She puts her palm up, silencing me.

"We will tell the elders your tale, although I believe you. Kitaico's fate will lie in their hands."

Just as quickly as I was whisked through to the bathing chamber, I'm brought back up to the main entrance door. Yissku opens it, and the guards bow to the flock of jewels with wide eyes.

They march me through the halls on a mission. The whispers of guards grow the closer we get to our destination. Finally, the bare-chested females demand that the doors in front of us open, and the guards stumble quickly, complying to their command.

The forceful rush of bodies behind me propels me into the room, creating a sensation of being swept away. Despite the scene I'm sure the women have created around me, even the elders lower their gaze.

The only set of eyes I see looking at us, *at me*, are Kitaico's.

Worry etches his face, his eyes filled with an unmistakable fear.

"Chancellor Hirouz." Yissku clears her throat before grabbing my wrist and forcing my palm up. "She is mated to this one…an unconsummated mating."

The delicate ring-encrusted finger points to my mate.

20 / more than honorable

MY STOMACH DROPS when I see the jewel raise Lena's marked palm for the elders to see.

This isn't what I wanted…I need more time to explain things, to make it right.

The air in the room grows still. The purple swirl on her human palm silences everyone in the room.

"Hopeful Kitaico, how can this be?" a lesser elder asks, his voice laced with uncertainty. "She is marked, but you are not?"

My skin prickles as my camouflage shifts colors to a muted gray. A wave of nervousness washes over me. The atmosphere in the room is thick with anticipation, and I can't hide my anxiety about explaining the status of my relationship with Lena.

"Because humans have nothing to sting with!" Lena twists her wrist from the jewel's grip, only to throw her hands up in the air. Her frustration is obvious from her tone. "God, our bodies are already so different from each other. Why is this surprising?"

My mate, who is clearly not an Andjin, is right. We are different, and I can't help but cringe as she gives the elders an attitude.

Was she like this in the cave when I couldn't understand her? A part of me worries if I even really know her at all.

But when she looks at me, a gaze so sweet that I can't break away, I know she is mine and I am hers.

"If she is marked, she must be compatible with our kind. The mating barb should only be present during ovulation." Chancellor Hirouz's voice cuts through the fuzzy feelings.

"My mate could carry my young?" The words slip from my lips, tasting almost as sweet as she does.

The council's shocked murmurs fill the space, but the room grows quiet when Hirouz stands.

"The human is marked, but we cannot allow you to claim her as your mate until you are found worthy. You are smart enough to understand this, Kitaico," he scolds.

"I don't need him to be found worthy. I just need *him*!" Lena begs, her voice cracking with desperation.

"Do you both swear, on the spirit of the Great Mother, that no breeding has occurred yet?" a deadly serious Hirouz asks.

I don't give a second for my mate to answer—I don't want to mince words.

"I haven't rutted Lena, despite the heats," I tell him truthfully. "My seed has never laid within her."

Chancellor Hirouz's foretentacles rub slowly over each other, as if he's deep in thought.

"I can't imagine the fortitude and willpower it took to resist a female in heat. Having gone through it with my own mate, I understand the hardship you must have endured." He pauses as if readying to say something profound—but Lena's voice cuts through that silence.

"I begged him to fuck me. He was more than honorable. Shouldn't that be proof enough of his worthiness?" The sound of her voice is filled with cracks, as if it were on the verge of shattering, like she knows she's fighting a losing battle.

"He has one last test," the chancellor says with less patience.

"If he passes that test, can we be together?"

"Your human body seems compatible with continuing the Andjin bloodline—"

"Is breeding all you care about? What if I loved him? What if we can't be apart without hurting…doesn't any of that matter?" Lena's fists are balled up at her sides as she cuts off Hirouz. I know I should remain humble and reverent in front of the elders, but I can't see her suffer.

I stand to my full height in the sight of the assembled elders and rush to Lena's side. Great Proving be damned.

I know she's my true mate.

My arms, and the brothers, grip her protectively as she unravels. She bites her lower lip to keep from crying, but the fat tears spill all the same.

"I will fight for her," I say, knowing that my only options are to keep Lena or die trying.

In a tender gesture, one brother softly caresses Lena's cheek.

"It isn't done this way!" a lesser elder shouts.

"Is this what our species has come to? By the Great Mother's grace." Another is astonished at our boldness.

More murmurs build before Chancellor Hirouz lifts his palm, demanding silence.

"Elders, we cannot comprehend the mysteries of the Great Mother. Nor can we deny that this strange creature has taken Kitaico's mating mark." He pauses like before, but not long enough to allow Lena to get a word in edgewise.

"You must complete your last task, but I know you know this. You have my word that once you are found victorious, that you will be found worthy of your human mate."

Lena's yelp of relief fills the chamber as she slumps into my arms and tentacles.

"We can be together," she coos as she tenderly peppers my face with kisses.

"Soon I will have you completely," I respond, my heart filled anew with a burning hope.

"Until then, the human will stay with the jewels. Her fellow females can teach her more about our culture," Hirouz says.

Lena nods quickly. "Whatever it takes."

"I will direct the medics to provide our human jewel with heat suppressants as well," the chancellor advises me with a knowing glance. "To make sure we don't stretch the hopeful's willpower any further than necessary."

"Wait, there have been heat suppressants this entire time?" She looks hurt, her eyes filled with sadness.

I lean in closer and quietly admit to her, "I had no idea they existed."

"It is not something we encourage the use of here on the Korlyan Moon. In fact, I've only seen it used when a newly mated Andjin's mate has died. It's the kind thing to do."

If Lena died…I couldn't go on.

"We have two days until the battle. I hope you survive, Hopeful Kitaico, for what it's worth. May the goddess keep you." The chancellor breaks his steely demeanor only for a moment to wish me well.

"Battle? Kitaico, what does he mean if you survive? What in the hell is this last test?" Lena is frantic.

I let out an inaudible sigh, knowing this moment was coming.

"Chancellor, may I have permission to spend the afternoon with Lena, to explain the Great Proving?" I ask humbly, gulping at the thought it might be the last time we're alone together.

Hirouz turns to the elders on either side of him, their disapproving glances not going unnoticed.

"This afternoon, until the rest of the jewels retire, you may converse in private with Jewel Lena. A guard will be posted outside the door, but I will allow you this."

I bow, knowing he's given us much more grace than I deserve. I'll wonder about his reasoning later.

The elders watch us silently, their wise eyes observing every move we make. Lena's worry is etched on her face, her brow furrowed and her lips pressed into a thin line. I can sense the fear radiating from her.

I hold Lena all the tighter, silently promising her we will face whatever comes our way as a united front. Our embrace is a silent reassurance, a gesture that I hope speaks volumes to these revered figureheads of my community.

I will win, I will claim Lena. There are no other options.

21 /

burning for me

LENA SWIGS the dark blue liquid from the small vial provided to her by the jewel's personal medic.

The heat suppressant should work instantly, or so I've been told. I'm still astounded such a thing even exists.

When the guard snaps the door shut behind us, I can't help but worry that maybe without the effects of my venom, she won't feel the same about me. I distract myself from that prospect of pain by surveying our surroundings.

The room is no better than a glorified cell, with no windows, and no furniture beyond the two plush, high-backed chairs that face each other in the small space. I almost wonder what this room is used for, but I'm preoccupied by the warm body that presses against me.

As if they know our mate needs to be soothed, the brothers instinctively reach for the weary-looking Lena. My arms soon follow.

As we stand, my mate slumps against me, her body as heavy as her heart, I think.

"What's the last test, Kitaico?" she mumbles into the crook of my neck.

"It doesn't matter, because I will win for you." I kiss her eyelids. The human gesture just seems right at this moment.

"I believe you, but my goal is to be prepared. I wasn't ready for most of what space has offered me. Some of it's been awful—but you, Kitaico, have been one of the best parts. Despite the heats, despite the situation we're in now, I love you." She grips her fingers into the muscles of my back, as if she's afraid she'll disappear.

My heart racing, I find the words to respond.

"I love you, too," I tell her, feeling completely surprised. "I never thought it was possible to feel this for someone without the mating sting. Even without the mark, or your venom, I know you're my mate."

I stroke my hand down her pink hair, which has faded since she first arrived.

"So, we both care about each other. You can't shoulder this fight alone. Tell me what to expect and how I can help you win." She pulls back, her brown eyes determined.

I suck my bottom lip between my fangs, trying to find the best way to break the gravity of our situation to this precious creature.

"The last test of the Great Proving is a gladiator battle against the hopefuls from my division." I lower my eyes. "The last Andjin male left alive will have the privilege to mate for life with one of the jewels."

"A battle to the death?" Fat tears are already cresting over my sweet Lena's lower lids.

"Yes, but save your tears for the others. Knowing you're what awaits me after victory gives me no choice but to succeed."

I know about my competition. For my entire life, we've been trained side by side, all while knowing that only one of us can complete the last challenge. They are, and always have been, my rivals, and for as confident as I'd like to say that I'm stronger…I don't know if I am.

So I must be more cunning and more ruthless than the other males. Knowing what I could lose is going to be the fuel I need to win.

"What happens if you—what if you don't come back to me?" The look on Lena's face kills me.

"I will."

"But I need to know, what happens to me? I don't want to be here without you." She puts her hands on my face, cupping my cheeks.

Pain, from her eyes, in my heart, pain is all I can feel.

"Y-you," I stutter, not wanting to think about the reality of a future without Lena. "You'll be treasured. As a jewel you'll be taken care of for your entire life. If you choose, in time, you can even mate another worthy male." The last part hurts to say, but I will be honest with Lena, because that's what she needs.

I will always give her what she needs.

The shaking starts in her shoulders until it takes over her whole body. My appendages wrap around her, trying to weather this storm of emotions my words have triggered.

I keep kissing her face, my tongue salty with the taste of her tears.

I'm taken aback when she clutches me, pressing her mouth to my lips, her tongue searching me for some kind of comfort.

Comfort is something I can give her.

I return her kiss, letting my hands run over the curves of her human form. We are different, but there's something so beautiful in the softness of her body and the slickness of her hair where tentacles should be.

Mine, always mine.

"I will win for you, to ensure we'll live a long and happy life together." I mumble between the clashing of our mouths.

"Forever?" Her hands run lower along my body.

"Until we're so old we can't move, until we decide to return to the Great Mother in the same second—I never want to be parted from you, even in death." The brother's cup her ass, lifting her body until I let my kisses trail down her chest.

I push the tattered woven top to the side, taking the hardening bud at the apex of her breast between my lips.

When Lena moans loudly, I muzzle my hand over her mouth.

"Quiet," I beg, "I need to comfort you. I need to give you this release. We can't let the guard hear. I can't leave you wanting."

Some faction of my psyche, no matter how much I don't want to admit it, knows this might be the last time we ever see each other.

"Won't you get in trouble? I want you, but I don't want to make this worse." She says warily as my hand slips from her lips, glancing at the door.

I don't answer her as my hands join my foretentacles at her ass. I carry her over to one of the chairs and set her down gently.

I promised the Chancellor that we hadn't mated, and it's true. I won't give her my seed until after I'm found worthy—and only if she'll accept it then.

I kneel at the altar of Lena, her arousal scent filling my nostrils and sending my blood to pump into the tips of every tentacle on my body.

For the first time since we met, I don't have to worry if my venom is what's making her crazy for me.

Lena burns for my touch right before my eyes, and every bit of her emotion is natural. She wants me, and I'll perish if I wait any longer to taste her.

The sound of her moans cuts through my concentration and one brother drags his tip right through her wet slit—lifting her skirt. Without warning, the other foretentacle covers her mouth once more.

"Shhh..." I whisper before I trail my tongue up her thigh. Lena bucks but stays quiet—despite needing to bite into the flesh of my tentacle to do so.

I don't even flinch because I will always give Lena what she needs, even if that's a bite of me.

My mouth waters as I lift the woven skirt I wrapped her in before the elder's arrival. Her scent intoxicates me, and I can almost feel my pupils dilating as I inhale.

"Lena, I want to use my mouth on your cunt, please let me." The smell of her alone has my cock hard and weeping. As she gazes down at me, my voice is filled with longing as I beg. "I need this, I need to taste you."

Lena pulls the brother from her lips, her voice quiet and as desperate sounding as I feel.

"Promise me you'll come back to me," she says as a chunky tear rolls down her cheek.

"I promise." It can't be a lie if you mean it with your whole heart, can it?

"I trust you, Kitaico."

The words feel weighty in the room. This is her answer to my promise and my request.

"Your trust is my honor to hold." I pull her slightly forward in her seat and whisper, "Will you open yourself to me?"

She pets a hand through my head tentacles before putting her hands on her knees and spreading them wide.

There must be no sight more enchanting, not even the promised afterlife by the Great Mother, than Lena on display before me.

My willpower breaks at her beauty.

I firmly grasp her hips, drawing her closer to my eager lips. As my tongue slides over her pearl, I can feel her body tense with pleasure, her breath quickening. I apply pressure, gently moving my rough tongue over her delicate sweet spot.

Lena bites her lip, suppressing the melodic sounds that I adore.

My hands grip into the flesh of her ass as I work my jaw over the apex of her sex. I can feel the left brother forcefully push past my chest and settle itself at her dripping entrance.

"Yes," she mutters softly, pressing her hips forward.

My Lena, without my venom, wants me.

I give her precisely what she craves—one brother penetrates her fervent and drawn cunt with haste. I replace my tongue with my fingers.

"So tight for my tentacle, I yearn for the day I earn your companionship. To have you milk my cock with these same muscles, I'd spill into you endlessly. The thought of you full and dripping with me, I can't imagine a sight more lovely."

As I speak, I can feel her motions become more frantic.

"So take me Kitaico, make me yours." Her whispers are rushed, her eyes hooded with pleasure as she looks down at me. "I trust you, I love you, give me everything."

"When I return, if you want me still, I will deny you no longer."

Lena's eyes roll back in her head as my tentacle balls up inside her, pushing against the spongy spot along her inner wall.

"Until I can make you my mate, when I return victorious, this moment of pleasure will sustain us both. You are the only sustenance I need."

I dive back to her pearl, stroking it slowly until I feel her shake.

"You'll come back," she mumbles, her body bouncing. "You'll come back and give me all of you."

I suck on her pearl, bringing it deeply between my lips. When my teeth graze the overstimulated flesh, she comes undone.

As she throbs and pulses around me, I gather her up in my arms.

"I will always come back to you," I whisper as I nuzzle the column of her throat. "Always."

I want to stay here with her forever, to put off our inevitable separation, but I know she'll be safe in the care of the other jewels. So I'll leave her after this bliss—boneless and content.

Using my knee, I knock on the door. When the guard opens

it, his skin shifts to a bright orange, his eyes blowing wide on his inhale.

His mouth moves, words unwilling to spill from them. I know he smells what we just did, but I don't care.

"I will take my mate to the jewels' quarters, for her to be in their care until I'm victorious," I tell him before he can get a word out. The male is flustered.

"Put the jewel down, you have no right—"

"She is my mate. I have every right," I say calmly before making my way down the hall. The bumbling guard follows, telling me how wrong I am for touching a precious jewel. How he'll rat me out to the council of elders.

But how could Lena in my arms feel anything but right?

"One day, you'll have a mate. Then you'll understand how I can fear nothing but her loss. Do what you must," I mutter.

The guard stops at my response, maybe not used to a hopeful's insolence. As he watches me stroke my mate's hair, something snaps into place. He sighs, defeated, and shoos me down the corridor.

"Get her there quickly and join the other hopefuls for tomorrow's battle in the holding tanks. They should arrive tonight." He frowns deeply and turns, making his way back to his post.

Looking at an almost sleeping Lena, I know that I have no choice but to return. I will spill my opponent's blood in the stadium tomorrow.

"I love you," I tell her one more time, just in case it's my last.

22 /
traditions

I SHOULD OPEN MY EYES, I should beg him not to leave me—*but I'm a coward.*

I'll stay in this hazy place between bliss and sleep and push the feeling that Kitaico is being forced to abandon me down deep.

When his lips brush my brow, staying detached feels all the harder. I know he understands because he doesn't push me back into reality.

With the utmost care, he sets me down onto a velvety surface, like a feather gently landing on a cloud. As soon as I catch a whiff of the incense, I am certain that I have arrived in the jewel's chambers. Kitaico will leave me here and go fight in his battle to the death.

"Sleep, sweet Lena. Don't worry, I'll return to you," he whispers.

With his touch slipping away, I grit my teeth and bite the inside of my cheek to suppress the urge to cry out. As his footsteps fade away, a wave of sadness washes over me, and I can't hold back the tears any longer.

When I finally am brave enough to open my eyes, the golden tiles nestled in the ceiling are blurred. The lights are dim, only a few glowing orbs float around the space like some kind of alien night light.

When I sit up, I bring my knees against my chest. I'm reclining on one of the chaise lounges, just like the Andjin females were doing when I first spotted them.

To think that I'd be having a breakdown where one of those decadently ornamented creatures sat hours earlier is laughable.

Without a doubt, I'm in the midst of a crisis. Just like my heats earlier, emotions surge through me uncontrollably. My love for that sweet alien is something I had only just realized, and now the fear that I might lose him. My adoration and terror collide within me like a speeding freight train, leaving me completely shattered.

I let out a groan, and my stomach twists and turns with unease. The pain is a sharp, stabbing sensation in my body.

Why the fuck didn't I hold him one more time?

My body sways as I rock back and forth in my seat, trying my best not to feel the anxiety. I need to be strong—but I can't.

I didn't think I would get a happy ending, and maybe I still won't, but the fact that I'm so close to it and it might be ripped away? Despair, it's the only thing I can think to call this feeling.

I don't know if I can be strong anymore.

As I wipe my stinging eyes with my forearm, a snot bubble unexpectedly bursts in my nostril. Through watery vision, I spot Yiskku's imposing figure in the arched doorway.

The shoulders of the gown are still encrusted with gems, but she's dressed in softer clothing than the chains of before. The sheer linen-looking fabric is wrapped around her body and tied with a golden sash.

She cocks her head, judging the sorry scene I'm making of myself, I assume.

"It's a hard night for all of us, you know," she says, a little abrasive.

"He's my mate," I say between the breaths that keep getting stuck in my throat.

"And they're ours." She strides closer. "Even the ones who lose the last challenge are our friends. This is never easy."

"You know them?" I ask, surprised that the jewels would be allowed such close contact with other males after seeing how cloistered their living arrangements are.

"Of course we do, how bizarre it would be to mate a stranger —" Yissku stops herself and bites her lip, her small fang hanging over the edge of her mouth.

"Yeah, bizarre," I say sarcastically as my heart breaks for my mate, who was just a stranger not so long ago.

"We—we are allowed to socialize with the hopefuls at orga-nized events." She stutters slightly, regaining her confidence. "There are several festivals and dances throughout the celestial cycle. Each jewel has her favorite hopeful…we're rooting for someone too." Her face is sad, but I can't bring myself to ask her who *her* hopeful is. I'm going to have to detach myself from anyone in the final challenge who isn't *mine*.

"Then why do it? Can't you just pick a mate on your own? I don't understand all this ridiculous nonsense—"

"I'm sure there are things on your planet I wouldn't under-stand, but that doesn't make your traditions anymore nonsense than ours." Yissku crosses her arms. "Things are the way they are for a reason."

"A reason? So you can be a prize?" I scoff.

"No, so that we can be protected, so that the breeding pool is strong. There are fewer and fewer females born every year— we have to do something!" She gestures broadly with her hands.

"But people are dying? How is that fair?"

"It's not fair, but it's what we do to make sure the jewels are safe. We are the life bringers, and without us, the Andjin would die out. But there's beauty and love here on the Korlyan Moon, even though it's hard fought."

She sits next to me, placing a hand on my thigh. I'm taken aback that she's trying to comfort me. I thought I was in line for a scolding.

"But death is the only option?"

"Death isn't the only option—but the hopefuls who choose to continue the Great Proving would rather risk everything for a chance at love. We all make our own choices. The males can choose to serve the Great Mother as celibate temple guardians, or find pleasure in each other or madness as exiles, or fight for the right to mate a jewel—at least they have choices." Her shoulders drop, her skin flashing a depressed gray.

"We don't have a choice, do we?"

"No, the jewel's choice was made by the Great Mother at our birth."

"Couldn't you become an exile too?"

She laughs sardonically. "I have no skills to survive in the wilderness. The elders make sure of that."

"So you're just as trapped as me then."

"No, whatever happens, you've known love—that might be more than I ever get."

A moment of realization dawns on me. She thinks I'm the lucky one.

And maybe she's right. Somehow, despite being light-years apart, Kitaico and I found each other.

We still have a chance at happiness, all hope isn't lost yet.

I grip her hand on my leg, trying to convey my sadness for her, but my hope for both our futures, all at once.

"I'm sorry, Yiskku. Tonight, can we dream of a happy tomorrow?" I force a smile to grace my lips.

"Only if you promise to cry quietly," she scoffs. I have a sense that Yiskku isn't used to opening up. She would fit in great in the Midwest. "The other girls' crying was keeping me up already—

we'll sleep here, it's much less depressing." She shoots me a tiny grin.

I wipe my cheeks once more for good measure, take a deep breath, and recline on the chaise.

"Thank you," I whisper.

"For what? Go to sleep, control your emotions, human," she says with her eyes closed. She's trying to shrug off her attempts at comforting me, as if it's no big deal.

But it is.

I'm sure for some humans a kind word doesn't go very far— but for me, a Midwestern gal? Kindness is a fucking king, even if it's given begrudgingly or played down.

"For giving me some hope that if something happens to Kitaico, that I could still find a friend here. Except for him, space has been cruel to me."

"Whatever happens, and I'll remind you we're still hoping for the best, you'll be safe here—treasured even. You're a jewel after all," she says softly. "Now shut up and go to sleep."

brothers in fate

THE HOLDING tanks are as depressing as my mood. What should have been a bittersweet reunion with my fellow hopefuls, the males I grew up with, is instead a morose reminder of all the lives I'll have to take to make it back to Lena.

I shouldn't have left her in tears, but I had no choice. She'll be safe with the jewels, even if I'm gone.

I'm glad my division of hopefuls is the first in the arena. I want to do what needs to be done to find my way home to her. I don't need to see more of my friends die before that.

I take a moment to let my eyes adjust to the dim lighting of the ancient chamber. Dust particles float in the air. As I lean against the stone walls, the rough texture scrapes against my skin. It serves as a stark reminder that I am once again thrust into the Great Proving, devoid of any modern comforts, including my clothing. I protectively cup my cock and mating crest, to shield it from the floor's rough surface.

"What's she like?" asks a voice filled with curiosity from the other side of the room.

It's Guion, his small body hunched against the wall, much like my own. Quiet little Guion. He has always been kind to me, even if all of us just feel bad for him. Even Aekaz told him to go to the temple and become a guardian—but he stayed as a hopeful. He will never win in the final challenge. I wonder what it must be like to know when your life will end.

"She's perfect," I say, feeling my tiredness as I rub my hand over my face. Her tear-streaked face is imprinted on the back of my eyelids. I have to shake the painful image from my mind.

"They should have put you to death on the spot. It's a disgrace that you're allowed to continue—your spawn will be an abomination to the mighty Andjin line," a vicious voice echoes from a deeper part of the chamber.

Even before he steps into the light, I can recognize him by sound alone. Only the cruelest of the hopefuls possessed that voice dripping with such disdain.

As Aekaz, the brute, emerges from the shadows, his massive presence fills the room. His body, larger than life, seemed almost comical in its exaggerated proportions.

While the rest of us worked on the skills we'd need to care for a jewel, Aekaz worked on his vanity muscles. Even his foretentacles ripple with unnatural bulges.

"Don't worry your overinflated biceps about such matters, Aekaz. You'll be long dead before you even have to worry about seeing my young." I wave him off. There's no use explaining to him I would never breed Lena before I was found worthy.

I had hoped that he'd have gone crazy with no one to boast to. My dreams of hearing about an exiled Aekaz are dashed.

"Me, dead? Surely, you must have me confused with every other sorry soul in this room. I was born to win, to conquer you all." He beats his fist over his chest, his normally orange skin flashing an aggressive red.

"I'm surprised you don't plan on defeating every other

hopeful division this year too. Would you even be happy with just one mate?" I scoff at his brash posturing.

"Isn't this about p-protecting a jewel and continuing our s-species?" Guion stutters. I'm surprised he's even addressed Aekaz. He does his best to avoid contact with such a bully.

"Yes, *my reward*...but don't think I won't find joy in extinguishing each of your lives—the Great Mother has built me to defeat you." He grins as he flexes.

"I'd let you kill me first just so you stop flapping your lips," Roinsi, the funniest of us all, groans.

"You'll die when I decide, no sooner, no later," Aekaz barks as he drops to the ground and begins a series of pushups that I'm sure he'll loudly count for all of us to hear.

"Save it for the arena. There's no point in spending some of your last moments arguing," I say, exasperated.

"Kitaico?" Guion asks.

"What?"

"If I am found to be the victor, will I be assigned to the human...since that's who you're fighting for?"

His question is innocent, as is his hope that he could ever stay alive with the three of us as competitors. The sharp pain of my fang piercing the inside of my cheek serves as a physical reminder to suppress my instinctive need to protect my mate.

"No, she is already mated. It would be impossible." I get out through my gritted teeth.

"Well then, shouldn't there be two winners? There will be one more jewel than there are hopeful divisions. Why can't they simply allow you both to be together?" He's sad for me, I realize. Despite his impending doom, he wants me to be with my mate.

"It's...it's just not done that way. I'm not sure what the elders will do with the remaining jewel if I win, but we must trust in their guidance," I say, almost as if to convince myself of it, too.

"It's not fair," he whispers.

"No, I suppose it's not."

It was as if time stood still, and for just a moment, I could vividly recall the innocent days of our youth. While our personalities are much the same, it is Guion who holds onto the belief that there exists a way out of this situation where none of us have to harm the others.

I wonder if Aekaz could have been a decent person if the circumstances were different. Could we have been friends in another life?

As if he knows what I'm thinking, he stills and stops his counting at Guion's admission.

"But we'll do our duty. We'll fight for the chance to protect a jewel. And if we fail, may the Great Mother welcome us into paradise with open arms." Without a hint of humor, Roinsi has clearly already accepted all our fates.

The room is bathed in a warm glow as the first rays of sunlight filter through the skylight, serving as a reminder that the time in the arena is approaching. The end of life as we know it looms over us, and the grim reality of death awaits all but one.

"May the best male for the jewels win," I whisper.

24 /
hide and seek

THE OTHER JEWELS have dressed me in what Yiskku says is "befitting my station."

I stand there, with golden chains cascading over my shoulders and bare chest. To accessorize further, they painted my nipples with a coat of gold when I declined their offer to pierce them. It sounds fun, don't get me wrong, but fun is the furthest thing from my mind. Pierced nipples or not, just like all the other women, my chest is exposed to the world.

"If Kitaico prevails, let me—the sensations will be worth it in the long run," Yiskku whispers to me. Her tone, always tinged with annoyance, reminds me of what having an older sister might feel like.

Is she annoyed by my mere existence? Of course, but I think she wants the best for me all the same.

"I think he likes my nipples just fine," I laugh, but a wave of guilt washes over me, instantly dampening the lighthearted moment.

As we walk down the hall, the metal censer swung by the

Andjin religious leader releases a cloud of fragrant incense smoke.

I won't allow myself to be happy until I can be sure he's safe. With a determined look on my face, I take on a solemn attitude as we are guided down the hall toward the arena viewing tower, my heart beating faster with each step.

I don't know if the onlookers are a regular occurrence or if the Andjin are simply curious about the human usurper, but the sight of the crowds lining the halls as we pass by is unsettling. They crane their necks to get a glimpse, some bowing their heads as we walk by.

Despite the reverence in which I'm now being viewed, it can't help but make me think of the past.

In a humid and smoky space nightclub, the leering aliens gathered around, their curious gazes darting back and forth, consuming me with their eyes as I writhed in my security bubble, my system loaded up with aphrodisiacs. Nothing more than meat. I was something to be ogled.

Even though the Andjin keep telling me that to be a jewel is to be revered, it's been a living hell to be separated from Kitaico. The heat suppressants work, thankfully, but I know for sure that my feelings for him run deeper—the kindhearted goofy alien really is my mate.

And this march to the arena is killing me—to know that I might never touch him again. I can only pray that this isn't Kitaico's funeral procession.

My feet slow as we approach the viewing bay for the arena, and I feel warmth at my palm.

When I look down, Yiskku's pale chartreuse hand is wrapped around my own.

"Come, whatever his fate is, we'll know soon," she mutters as she drags me through the doorway.

"How can you do it? How can you watch them die?" My breath sticks in my throat like paste, thick and bitter.

"Because they're fighting for us, and it would be shameful

not to honor that fight." Her eyes shine with some hidden sadness.

"If he dies, I can't —" I struggle to get the words out.

"You're a jewel. Despite your species, you are the best of anyone on the Korlyan Moon. You will be taken care of, but you must be brave." As her face shifts, a stony mask settles upon her emotions, hiding any sign of vulnerability. "Come."

Yiskku deposits me in a chair next to Chancellor Hirouz. I gulp down my sadness, clearing my throat and try my best to keep it together. I can feel a small polite smile creep over my lips, but I know my eyes are vacant. My best midwestern dissociation face settles in. It must unnerve the chancellor, because at first his brows knit. But his expression softens as he hands me a glass of something strong smelling.

"Thru'ik liquor, to calm your nerves," he says plainly.

I want to hate him for putting Kitaico and me in this position, but like almost everyone else I've encountered here, he's kind. I sniff the cup, and it reminds me a bit of vodka. I swallow it down eagerly, hoping it tastes like home, but the alcohol sears my insides, causing me to gasp for breath. It's much stronger than I thought.

"Th-thank you," I stutter. Despite the taste, I wish there was more in the cup. I'd do anything to dull the anxiety right now.

"I didn't realize humans imbibed in such quantities," he laughs under his breath.

I can only imagine his face if he saw how well I could shotgun a beer—almost as much as I want his reaction with what I say next.

"This is barbaric. I want you to know that. I'm only complying because I have no other option. If he dies—"

"How could he? He's got something none of the other hopefuls in his division have." He raises a hand to silence me. I wonder if that's rude in their culture.

"What does he have? Did you give him something, a weapon to gain the upper hand?" My heart swells. Could the chancellor want Kitaico to win—could he be rooting for us in secret?

"No, he has you, a mate."

My stomach hits the ground. I want to scream.

What if I'm not enough to get him through this? What then?

But my screaming and tears haven't gotten me anywhere yet, have they?

So instead, I face forward and plan all the ways I'll take revenge if the worst happens. And what a view I'll have. The dichotomy of high and low tech on the planet continues to astound me.

Despite feeling like a fantasy concubine, draped in gems and golden chains, the viewing window onto the arena looks like something out of the movie *Minority Report*.

Translucent screens float and shuffle along the convex and bulging window. They run what I assume are stats of the hopefuls. Some of the smaller screens are zoomed in on a set of stone doors. The arena seems to be built of the same lava rock that Kitaico's cave was.

Given the large windows, I assumed it would be an underwater battleground…but it's not. There are puddles of bubbling water, like the hot springs Kitaico took me to.

The arena is smaller than I expected. I don't know why I thought it would be like *The Hunger Games*, where they had a basically unlimited expanse of space, but it's much more like a Roman gladiator pit. There are a few large plants and piles of rocks and debris scattered throughout.

To the farthest side opposite our large window, the crater opens into the ocean, waves lapping at the black sand. The open water spreads out as far as my eyes can see beyond that.

Beneath us are rows and rows of bubbled windows.

And here we sit at the top, in box seats to the bloodbath. My stomach twists, not wanting to bear the gruesome ritual these people hold dear.

Once I let the grisly thought leave my mind, I realize something else about the space. The entire arena appears to be in a long-dead volcanic crater. The Andjin have carved out their homes in this rocky mountain, running tunnels and rooms like ants in a hill.

Yiskku comes back and takes a seat in the chair next to me, sandwiching me between her and the chancellor.

Some dissonant instrument sounds as she once again grabs my hand.

"Are you ready?" she whispers, eyes glued to the screens with the doors.

"No."

Despite my protest, my attention is drawn to the screens as the heavy double doors swing wide.

Four males, all so different, stand tall. The screen lights up with Kitaico's face, and he winces as a bright pink light washes over him.

Just as if it's his cue, the chancellor rises from his seat and confidently approaches the floating screens. Grabbing a small circular disk, he places it over the column of his throat.

"May the hopefuls bring honor to their families. We thank them for their sacrifice." His voice booms through the hidden speakers in the room. "May the best male overcome his opponents. At the signal, you have five minutes to take your starting positions."

Kitaico's face, visible through the screen, displays complete resolve. But so do the faces of his companions.

One of them, right beside Kitaico, stands out because of his immense size. His biceps are unbelievably huge, larger than my entire waist. There's a cruelty to his face as he smiles for the cameras. It's so incredibly unnerving that I look away. I can feel his gaze burning holes at me through the holo screens.

"That's Aekaz," Yiskku whispers in my ear. "His muscles draw the blood away from his brain, do not worry."

For as much as I want to laugh, I can't. Stupid or not, he is impressively terrifying.

A single note comes through the loudspeakers again, and my heart is filled with dread as the arena goes black and all the lights are shut off. A measured beeping, I assume to count down the time, picks up its pace.

When the tone sounds so fast that it becomes constant, the lights return and the arena is empty, save for the brute of an Andjin standing in exactly the same place as before.

For a moment I assume the worst, that he's somehow already killed everyone, until Yiskku whispers, "They're hiding in plain sight," and points to a few of the outcroppings of rocks and brush that dot the arena.

I see nothing until Aekaz rushes the rocky pile to his left. When he grabs the smallest of the hopeful's neck, the little one's skin shifts back to his normal green color. He thrashes in his grip, his longer head tentacles reaching back up for Aekaz's throat.

When the tip of one appendage skirts by Aekaz's lips, he opens his mouth and bites down. His fangs sink into the muscular tube of flesh.

The sound of his screams reverberates in my ears as I witness the slow decay of the limb, the venom spreading like an ominous darkness. His anguished cries make it seem almost compassionate when Aekaz snaps his neck. The green body drops to the black ground, his head lifelessly bouncing off the pile of rocks as he does.

I knew the Andjin venom was deadly...but I didn't realize it was that incredibly gruesome.

Aekaz licks his fang as he steps over the fallen hopeful's corpse, pulling his shoulders back as he searches for his next target.

He walks slowly and deliberately through the battleground. His nostrils flare as he stalks, stopping at any place that appears it might make a good hiding spot.

I lean into Yiskku and ask, "Why is it taking so long? He seems to have found the first male easily."

She pulls her lips back over her petite fangs, her face incredulous.

"His camouflage was terrible. Could you really not see him?"

"Nope, guess my human eyeballs just suck," I pout.

"Kitaico and Roinsi are much better in the art of evasion than poor Guion was," she says sadly.

"Why didn't Aekaz hide?"

"It's the way of things, the hopeful deemed the strongest hunts the others. It is a point of pride among our males to win at a disadvantage."

"I'm over male pride." I slump further into my seat.

I wish I was strong enough to look away from the screens, but I can't. As Aekaz throws boulders bigger than a midsize sedan around the arena, I'm transfixed.

Where are you, Kitaico?

Unfortunately, even I can spot him when the burned tip of his foretentacle, *the one I shot off,* comes into the camera's frame.

The portion of skin near the most damaged bit pulses yellow, as if it can't change like the rest of his hide. The burn mark stays the color he normally is.

"You fool." Aekaz's voice is broadcast through the arena as he grabs Kitaico's damaged appendage.

But Kitaico doesn't thrash like his first victim. Instead, he swipes his foot around, kicking out the other hopeful's legs.

As Aekaz drops to the dirt, Kitaico scrambles up the nearby rock, jockeying for a better position. But the brute jumps back up to his feet, looking up at my mate and laughing with his whole body.

"Having the higher ground will do nothing to stop me," he says before rushing Kitaico like hell on wheels, scrambling up the side of the rocks.

Despite Kitaico's defensive stance, when Aekaz's hand grips his arm, he can do little but try to stay as far back as his reach allows.

"I'll be sure that your mate is well taken care of," he tells my alien, his vicious voice dripping from the speakers.

The combination of the glint in his eye, his grip on Kitaico's arm, and seeing what he did to the first male has my vision tunnelling.

I think I scream when Aekaz spins my mate around, pushing his chest into the pile of rocks as he pins him down, using his knee to hold Kitaico's arm tightly against his back.

I can almost make out the feeling of the many hands that must be supporting me, but through the blur of tears, I cannot bring myself to avert my gaze. My body feels like it's operating on its own, separate from my mind.

Kitaico's shoulder muscles twist and his jaw clamps as he tries to get out from under the giant Andjin's grip.

Aekaz turns his eyes skyward, ignoring the struggling male beneath him. He doesn't even break a sweat keeping his hold. Cockily, he looks directly into the camera before leaning down and whispering into my mate's ear.

"You've met your fate, and his name is Ae—"

25 /
no antidote

AEKAZ'S KNEE presses into the space between my shoulder blades, forcing me against the rough outcropping of rocks. Behind me, the brothers grapple with his leg, their frantic efforts to dislodge him proving futile against his unyielding strength.

His grip is unshakable, trapping my arm behind my back and leaving me helpless to escape no matter how much force I exert with my free hand.

I've been bested by Aekaz.

He's taking his time, showing off to the arena. I feel like a prize kill, about to be dispatched by its hunter.

I know he's yelling at the crowds, but I can't make out what he's saying because all I can hear is a muffled scream through his nonsense. The sound is far away, but I'd know the tenor of Lena's voice anywhere.

The pain behind it is something I haven't heard before, though. A strange sensation flows through me. My body reacts to her cry, and some kind of hot power courses through my veins.

My mate is in danger.

I buck, barely lifting my shoulder off the ground. A guttural sound leaves my throat as I sputter against the burning in my body. The pain that radiates from the spot where my arm connects to my body is blinding. But I fight through it. I do it for Lena, to protect her, to keep her safe. Growling into the sandy surface of the rocks, I feel the black granules sticking to my spit on my chin.

She is mine and mine alone, and I refuse to leave her.

Another wave of adrenaline courses through me, igniting a fiery heat in my chest. As I push my body beyond its breaking point, my shoulder pops free from the joint, sending a shock-wave of agony through my entire being. Free from the restraints, I'm able to maneuver my body smoothly out from under Aekaz's knee.

Instinctively, the cocky bastard reaches for me with his hand, like a spoiled child seeking a favorite toy as it rolls away.

I don't hesitate this time, and neither do the brothers. They bind themselves like whips onto his wrist, dragging the huge male forward. He stumbles over a particularly jagged rock, his side scrapping against it hard. I can smell the blood as it blooms from the wound on his torso.

I can't tell if he's stunned at the injury, or at the battle swinging in my favor, but he freezes all the same.

His eyes go wide, and his skin flashes the color of fear when he's unable to stop me as I bite down on the side of his palm, engaging the venom in my fangs. I deliver the killing blow.

He's stock still as the brothers release him, as if he's unable to believe that unremarkable Kitaico has ended him. I jump back out of his reach, far enough that his foretentacles won't be able to bring me in for retaliation.

"I'm sorry it ends like this. I only do what I must to protect my mate," I mutter, honestly regretful to take his life.

I know in a different world he might have been kinder.

Being part of the Great Proving has shown me what it can do to a male, how it can kill any kindness in a person. What would I be if not for Lena? Would I be driven to madness in the pursuit of a jewel?

Aekaz's flesh darkens as my venom works through his bloodstream. The blackening veins trail up his palm and wrap around his wrist. I regret what I must do when the pain has him falling to his back, clutching his hand against his broad chest.

I find no joy in this murder, but his screams mean nothing compared to Lena's. I would kill a hundred hopefuls if I meant I could take her home.

As I turn my back to the dying male, I know that I still have Roinsi left to find.

Just one more step and then I'll be home.

I'm only able to take a single step away before I hear a splash. I pivot, thinking my final remaining opponent has jumped from the shoreline and is making his attack.

But my mouth drops open as I see the egg Lena arrived at being dropped into the ocean. But it's not Lena that's inside. It's a different human woman. She pounds her fist against the side of the egg as it sinks below the surface.

There's a whoosh of wind as Roinsi reveals himself and rushes past me, arching his body and diving into the waves toward the strange human in her egg.

Turning my eyes skyward, I inhale sharply. Human eggs are dropping from the sky all around the arena. They hit the water hard, but are quickly sucked down under the waves by the strong rip currents.

There's so many of them, all scared and being tossed around inside their pods.

I only break my focus on the sky when there's a scream behind me. It's Aekaz. Turning back, I see his gray face looking down at his own severed hand. The trail of blood leads me to believe he's cut it free from his arms using the same sharp rock that pierced into his side.

He must have sawed it off to stop my venom's progression. Viscous fluid spirts from the gore-capped joint. His foretencale wraps itself around his elbow to staunch the blood loss.

The pale Andjin male pays me no mind as he grits his teeth and bursts into a sprint to the water. Every step looks like agony as he trails his blood across the black sand. He reaches the water and escapes the arena. Whether to die on his own terms or live as an exile, I'm unsure…but he's gone all the same.

When the eggs have stopped falling from the sky, and the last of the humans slip below the waves, I face the chancellor's window.

This madness must end. Roinsi knows this, he's already trying to save the humans. I know it too, but I won't risk losing Lena to do so.

My good arm thumps on my chest as I yell my plea up to the top of the arena.

"We must protect the jewels!"

There are a few beats of disconcerting silence before I hear Chancellor Hirouz clear his throat.

"The last challenge will be delayed. Save the females!" he announces.

I can barely make out his window from here, but I see the shape of my mate as she drops to her knees beside him, tugging at his robes, chest heaving.

She's okay.

Distraught, but here. She's not in danger, I realize. The scream before must have been one of grief as I was about to die.

We need each other.

The chancellor lifts the Lena-shaped shadow and moves her away from the window.

Males, both those mated to jewels and the temple guardians who thought themselves fated to be alone forever, pour from the same doors I walked through moments ago.

They all rush the shoreline, descending into the waves. By the time I make it into the water, groups of males are already pulling the first of the eggs onto the shore.

As I dive into the salt depths, spearing my body toward the closest human, I wonder what part the Great Mother had in this.

Is the time of the Great Proving over? Is her divine power what pushed me to bear the pain of my dislocated arm? I tuck the useless limb against my body. One brother lashes it to my side to reduce my drag, and the other foretentacle wraps around the smooth plastic egg along with my good arm. The scared human retreats to the far side. Through the pod, I lock eyes with Roinsi, I know we both wonder if the challenge is truly over, or if this rescue mission is just a temporary pause for one of us on our way to death's door.

He nods to me, and we both kick, stopping the pod's descent and bringing the terrified human closer to the surface.

my destiny

MY HAND SNAGS on the golden chain draped around my shoulders as I go to wrap a blanket around one of the shivering humans who's being brought inside. I yank at it, letting the golden links split and fall to the floor. I could't care less. The only thing driving me right now is making sure the girls are safe and that I can see my mate again.

"What's going on?" the scared woman mutters, clutching the blanket tightly around her bruised body. "Did the Deenz sell us?"

She looks down to my garb and quickly looks away from my gold- painted nipples.

"No, you're safe, deep breaths." I breathe with her, hoping that she's able to calm down.

I point to Yiskku, and push the girl toward her as even more bubble babes are brought into the large dining hall. The space is set for a victory dinner for whatever hopeful pulled through, but now it seems more like a disaster triage ward.

"Go with her, she'll take care of you. I have to check on the other girls."

Half the women I've talked to don't even have a translator chip installed, and some are still in their street clothing. These girls are fresh off their abductions...it's even more confusing why the Deenz would drop them into the ocean. I had assumed that I was just too used up to be worth the investment anymore. But why abandon "fresh cargo," as they had called me right after my abduction.

"There's just so many, please, let me back out. I can't let my mate's people suffer!" an Andjin shouts from the hall. It's not any male, but mine. Kitaico is pushing a medic away from inspecting his shoulder.

He doesn't see me when I come up behind him, but when I wrap my arms around his waist, pressing my chest into his back, he stills and stops his arguing.

"Lena?" His voice cracks and he spins, gripping the back of my neck tightly and pulling my face into his. Our kiss is frantic and tastes of sweat and sand—but I can't stop.

"I didn't..." He pulls back every few seconds to speak. "...think that I would see you..." He kisses my eyelids. "...again."

I pull away and break our kiss, relief filling my heart.

"Not an option," I whimper as tears stream down my cheeks and the brothers grab at any soft bit of skin they can find.

His face drops when he sees me cry, and he goes to hug my body against his, but winces when his injured arm's hand goes limp.

"Stop." I put my hand up and turn to the medic, whose face is something between confusion and disgust. Aliens don't kiss, I remind myself.

"Can you fix him up first?" I ask the medic, whose foretentacle scrubs over his face before he huffs and gets to work resetting Kitaico's joint.

My alien winces as his arm is popped back into place, and for a moment I worry he might pass out as his eyes roll back. Kitaico recovers quickly, though, as the brothers still haven't released me, using my body for support.

"Don't use that arm for the next few days if you're able," the medic tells him authoritatively before moving onto a group of more badly injured human women. Some of them got pretty beat up on the drop.

"We did it," I whisper into his ear as I use one of the emergency blankets that's been provided to create a sling for his arm.

"I still haven't proven my worth. The final battle is merely delayed, isn't it?" Kitaico's brows knit in confusion.

"You haven't heard?" I ask, realizing how stupid that sounds as soon as I say it. "Of course you haven't heard, you've been rescuing women while injured."

"Heard what?"

"Chancellor Hirouz spoke with the emperor after the challenge was cut short. It's been decided that we need every male on the planet to help care for the refugees."

There's a delay between my words and the realization, and when it finally hits him, a broad grin spreads across his yellow cheeks.

"We get to be together?" My mate's voice cracks.

"Yes," I say softly.

Kitaico's face wavers from awed delight to a look of resolute failure.

"Without the Great Proving, how can I prove to you I'm a worthy mate? You deserve someone worthy." Kitaico drops his brow and steps back from me as far as the brothers will let him.

"Stop that." I swat at him before pulling his body back to my own. "You've proven yourself to me over and over again. You saved my life from the scripiat, you made sure I was fed, you tended my wounds, you protected me from the exiles…you were going to die for me, Kitaico. There's nothing left to prove. If anything, I need to prove that I'm worthy of your love…because I fucking love you. Kitaico, I accept you as my mate."

"She knew," he whispers with misty eyes.

"What, who knew?"

"The Great Mother…she knew I was destined for you. Everything that's happened since you dropped into my world has brought us closer together." Kitaico cups my cheek with his good hand, his skin shifting to a light purple color, and pulls me close. "You are my destiny."

Our lips crush together again, my body bursting with a heady cocktail of relief and affection.

Kitaico breaks the kiss, grabbing my hand and turning it over in his. His finger traces along the swirling purple mating mark.

"I only wish I could bear your mark, but I guess I'll have to get used to bucking tradition with a human as my mate, won't I?"

"Hold your horses. Who said I wasn't going to mark you?"

"I have no idea what a horse is, so I don't think I can hold them. But I might be confused in general—I thought you couldn't mark me?" He searches my wrist for some hidden mating barb.

"You'll see, but let's worry about all that later. Now let's help these women together." I double-check his sling before nodding my head in the direction of a new flock of scared humans.

"I can't believe we get a later," he mutters to himself as he follows me.

Later? I hope we get forever.

marked

I DEPRESS the button to the space that will be both mine and Lena's home. It's the same quarters given to all newly mated hopefuls, but it feels special.

Because it is, it's ours.

Lena rushes past me and nearly belly flops onto the bed, her limbs starfishing.

"This is so much softer than at the cave. I'm exhausted!" she groans into the pillow.

"I did my best." I try not to let my feelings about the nest I built get hurt. "When the time comes and we return to the nest, I'll build you something better."

I sit on the edge of the comfy bed. She turns her head, frowning at me with a look of compassion.

"That's not what I meant." She pushes herself up from the bed and places her warm hand over my thigh. "Anywhere I'm with you is home."

One of the brothers wraps around her waist and pulls her

tightly to me, and my cock, as predictable as the sunrise, hardens nearly instantly.

"Your cock is different than a human's, but it is so beautiful." She runs her hand through my mating crest, skirting the base of my shaft.

My body goes still, except for the brothers. I gulp, trying to will them to stop running their lengths up and down her sides.

"I am happy it pleases you," I say through gritted teeth.

"It would please me," she says, her eyes behind hooded lids, "if you told me what you liked. How do you want me to touch your cock, Kitaico?"

"I, uh, any way you want to—that's how I like it." My voice sounds squeaky in my own ears. I'm embarrassed when my cock bobs toward her hand, begging for contact.

"Is there something that someone else has done that's felt good?" She kisses me on the cheek.

Someone else? The thought of anyone but Lena makes my stomach roil.

"There has only been you."

Her eyes widen and her little pink mouth drops open.

"Only me? Kitaico, are you a *virgin*?"

A robed human woman flashes in my mind, my translator chip struggling to convey the meaning of the word.

"I don't understand this word."

"Have you had sex before?" Her face screws up as asks the question.

"Yes, you were there." Lena must have a terrible memory.

"No, I mean, have you ever put your penis inside anyone?" Her voice is gentle.

"I've never had a mate, no. I hope you'll let me, though." I try to ignore my throbbing cock as I answer her.

"Oh. Oh!" She seems flustered. "I mean, I guess it makes sense, I just didn't really think about it."

"So, there have been others for you, then?" I try not to look crestfallen.

"Yes, but not a mate. You are my first in that way." Lena bites her lip. "Does it bother you that you're not my first for other things?"

I think of it for a moment, not wanting to say the wrong thing. Do I like that there are males that have known the pleasures of my mate in the past? No. Do I find fault in her for it? Also no.

"It does not bother me. You bear my mark and you're here with me now. You are everything I've ever hoped for."

Her grin broadens at my mention of her mating mark.

"Speaking of marks, I had Yiskku drop something off for me!" She jumps from the bed, her excitement causing her to skip. I have to pinch the brothers to get them to release her as she moves. She scans our quarters until her eyes land on a medium-sized metal box on our table.

She grabs it and heads back toward me.

"What is it?" I hope it's something to distract my mind from my throbbing shaft.

Lena doesn't seem to pick up on my discomfort, her excitement over whatever lies in the box overshadowing my little problem. She lifts the lid, and inside there's a curious arrangement of objects. It contains a large bottle of antiseptic fluid, several piercing needles, sterile bandages, and what looks like a jar of mashed up nuite fruit.

"You'll have to explain." I tilt my head, trying to make sense of the box's contents. "Do you wish for me to pierce your nipples and then feed you a snack?"

Lena laughs so hard she nearly tips over onto me.

"I mean, that sounds fun, don't get me wrong, but no. I'm going to use this to mark you, like the marks I have. I'm going to tattoo you and give you a mating mark of your own." She beams at me, her smile pulled wide.

A mating mark of my own? My clever mate has found a way to claim me in the ways of our people.

"So, will you let me mark you as my own?" she asks in earnest.

When I look at her face, when I think of what she's offering me, my heart wants to explode.

"I would be honored to bear your mark, but how are these things going to help us do that?" I gesture to the box she holds.

"It's called a tattoo. I'll poke your skin with the needle and rub the nuite fruit into the cuts. Once it heals over, I hope it'll be permanent. From how the dye stained the cave walls, I think it should."

I narrow my eyes at her.

"I must love you if I'll allow you to stick me with needles and rub food in the wounds," I say half in jest.

"It'll be easy, promise. I haven't done a stick and poke tattoo since before my apprenticeship at the shop." She's giddy, so I don't ask her to elaborate on what shop she's talking about. "Should we do it tonight"—her eyes drift back down to my throbbing cock—"or maybe tomorrow, if you need me to…"

"No, I've waited long enough. I wish to be claimed," I try to say playfully, showing her my palm with a smile. I cross my leg over the other, willing myself to soften.

She plops down next to me, takes one of the bottles of sanitizer, and pours some onto her hands. She grabs my hand and rubs her wet palm onto mine. I watch with curiosity as she opens the sterile bandages and uses them to wipe one of the long, thin needles and the jar of purple goop. Lena opens the bottle of nuite fruit.

"I had them boil it. I think that's as close to sterile as we're getting, if that's okay." She looks somewhat nervously at the jar.

"I trust you."

She takes a deep breath and dunks one of the sanitized needles and eyes the skin of my palm, turning it from side to side.

"Would your mark look like my own, if I was an Andjin?" she asks.

"Yes, not every mating mark looks the same between all pairs, but mine would look just like yours."

She nods, sucking her lip between her teeth in an act of concentration. She grazes the tip of her the needle from the middle of my palm outward, matching the swirling mark I left on her own hand.

"That was fast," I say, shocked that it was so quick.

"I was just tracing the design out." She doesn't look up at me, but instead dips the needle back into the ink and places it at the center of the design.

"Ready?"

"Ready."

The needle enters my skin before I can even get the whole word out.

"People paid you to inflict pain on them like this?" I wince as she wipes at my throbbing palm. I can't believe that humans exchange credits for this kind of pain.

"Oh yeah, I made the big bucks." She rolls her eyes. "You know, for someone who nearly broke their own arm, I expected you to handle a little needle better than that."

"Whatever the pain, it is worth it," I whisper as she cleans the last of the nuite fruit from my palm.

There in neat purple lines punched into my skin, the swirling mark is so similar to the one I'd given Lena that I do a double take.

"It's the same as yours," I whisper softly as she wraps my hand.

It's as if she did have her own mating barb.

"I thought that was the whole point, wasn't it?" She laughs, gathering the used supplies into a neat bundle with the dirty bandages.

"It's beautiful all the same," I mutter under my breath as she searches for where to throw the waste.

I stand, walking over to a panel on the wall and hitting a button. The refuse chute pops from the carved stone.

"Thanks!" she says before depositing the purple stained pack down. Lena peers into the metal chute right as it snaps closed. She starts, clutching her hand to her neck, and looks back at me with a grin.

"There's a lot you're going to have to teach me, you know."

"Anything you want I will—"

"And there's things I want to teach you too, mate." She puts a finger on my lips, trailing it down my neck and between my pecs.

Even the brothers freeze with the anticipation of what Lena intends to teach us. My cock, which had gone soft under the pain my mate inflicted with her needle, swells quickly.

"I should have taken my heat suppressants when we got here. I can still take them if you want...but I thought maybe we deserved the whole mating experience—I can't give you my venom, but you can enjoy what yours has done at least." She runs her fingers back through my mating crest, its tentacles pulsating and grabbing onto her fingers.

"There will be no pretending. I've wanted to rut you since our first meeting," I admit, the tension of my hard cock starting to radiate a pulsing warmth through my body.

Lena's eyes blow wide, her heat taking over. I should have smelled the change in her body, known that she was ripening for me. But the *tattoo* distracted me just enough.

"Will you fuck me with that pretty cock?" She grips me at my base, squeezing in rhythm with the pumping blood.

"Ohhh." My breath comes in ragged pants, the brothers moving for her painted tits. I'm nearly ready to bust. "I...I don't know if I will last long."

"Good, as long as you promise me we'll go again. Will you fuck your cum deep into me?"

She's straddled my leg, and beneath her fine sheer skirts, her wet cunt finds friction over my thigh.

"I will, if you want my seed, if you want me to breed you…if you give me permission." I grab her hip, attempting to get some morsel of control.

She stops, the haze of her heat momentarily gone.

"Of course I do, if it's really even possible—I want all of you." She leans up, straining to meet my lips with her own.

"I'll give you everything then, my gift from the stars," I breathe right before I devour her with a kiss.

I lift her from my leg, setting her in my lap, but not entering her yet. I worry that she's too small for me, barely able to handle the girth of my tentacles, let alone my shaft.

As if reading my mind, the brothers move from her breasts down to her sex. One plays with her pearl while the other rubs her slickness along her opening.

Her muscles tighten as a tentacle works into her. When the resistance pressure feels like it might reach its peak, it slips inside her, testing her cunt's depth. When the other brother abandons her pearl to join its twin, she throws her head back, moaning my name.

Never was there a more beautiful sight in the entire galaxy.

first timers

THE HEAT SIZZLES through my skin. Every place our skin makes contact with one another is set ablaze. Being able to act on these feelings, to trust Kitaico, to want to give him everything, is fucking bliss.

It feels amazing, and that's even before his foretentacles enter me.

I dig my fingers into his pecs, throwing my head back and letting his name roll from my lips. There's a thrill inside me, knowing that he's never been with anyone before. That when he drives his fat cock into me, we'll both be experiencing things for the first time.

Even though he's a virgin, he'll be the only alien I've ever had.

The brothers stretch my channel, pushing my muscles to adjust to their girth. Kitaico works my clit with the thumb of his good hand. A tightening builds inside my core as the tentacles plunge into me all the more quickly.

"I can feel you tightening around me, breathe, relax—I want

to rut you, fuck you so deeply." Kitaico pants, locking eyes with me. His face is so earnest, his love so fucking pure. "Can I? Can I give you all of me?"

I respond by grabbing his weeping cock, my fingertips not meeting as I circle my hand around him. When I press it against the tentacles fucking me, they retreat, sliding out of me with a slurp.

I don't allow my pussy time to contract, not wanting to feel empty for a second. I drive my hips down but stop not long after his tip is inside me.

"I thought I was ready. Fuck, Kitaico." I wince as I work my hips slowly, rocking side to side, trying to take more of him inside me.

"You-you don't have to—" Kitaico's eyes are closed and every muscle in his neck is strained. He's trying so hard to be gentle, to let me set the pace.

"I need your help. I need you to fuck me, stretch me." I writhe atop him, not being able to push past the burn I feel on my own.

"What if I hurt you?" His hips give the tiniest thrust, as if unintentional.

"I don't care, I want all you, I want you to fill me up with you—"

The brothers loop under my thighs, drawing me up off his cock with a pop. Kitaico's eyes are hooded when he looks at me, and his jaw sets as he puts his hand on my low belly. As he pushes, the brothers slam me home. A sharp pinch jolts through me, causing my whole body to tense.

It hurts, but it's what I wanted, and as my body relaxes, the edge of pain shifts. I look down, and realize I'm fully over his shaft, the short tentacles around his cock thrum over the sensitive bundle of nerves at the apex of my legs. I pulse over him, and Kitaico lets out a grunt as he starts to withdraw from me.

"Slow, slow, slow," I whisper into his chest.

The slide of his cock, twisted and ridged, hits nerves inside me that I never knew existed.

"I, I can't keep this pace, I need—" He's lost to my body, a prisoner to my pussy.

When he exits me fully, my muscles clasp in vain over nothing.

I feel so empty that I can't bear it. I pull his hand to my clit, take a deep breath, and steady my resolve.

"Take what you need from me," I command.

Kitaico doesn't hesitate. His skin ripples deep purple as he stands and flips me onto my back. The soft bed groans as he kneels between my legs and whispers in my ear.

"The only thing I've ever needed is you."

He stands again, dragging my ass to the edge of the bed. Raising my left leg, he plants a kiss on the inside of my ankle. Leaving it up on his chest, he flicks my clit.

"Tell me if it's too intense."

The first stroke is slow, but with each exit he enters me all the faster, fucking me and eventually *rutting me.*

Words hold no meaning anymore, there's no blood left in my brain as I throb over his cock. Each stroke hits me like lightning, and my body has no idea what to do with the sensation.

The electricity builds at my center, and each upswing has me gasping. The last of the pain has ebbed away, and I root myself firmly in the blossoming pleasure.

"I am going to fill you up. I can't hold back anymore, I'm going to—"

Kitaico spasms, his dick jerking inside me. My mate's hot cum shoots deep.

The aftershocks of his orgasm have him pumping inside me until I can feel his seed slicking down my ass. Cock pulling free and resting between us on my tummy, he collapses on top of me. My body still hums with potential, my release so fucking close.

I want to stroke his hair, to tell him he did a good job. But before I can speak, the brothers find their way home.

Kitaico is barely conscious, his body heavy on me. That doesn't deter the brothers.

One tentacle is already pushing inside me as the other teases my backdoor. The brother at the rear is slippery with something, and I realize that it's using the cum that leaked from my pussy as lube.

What a considerate sentient tentacle.

"Oh," I say with surprise.

That's another first for me, and I don't hate it.

After fitting my mate's thick cock inside me, I find that I'm able to accommodate a tentacle in my ass rather easily. The slip and slide of the brothers inside both my holes is almost over-stimulating, the powerful muscles pumping against the barrier of skin between them. The nerves of my virgin rosebud are firing on all cylinders, adding to the throbbing of my pussy.

I thought I would never feel fuller than when he fucked me with his alien cock, but this is a new sensation altogether.

When Kitaico wakes, he doesn't miss a beat. He trails kisses along the column of my throat as his tentacles slide back and forth inside me.

"You fill me up so well," I whimper as he reaches between us for my clit.

The cord inside me breaks when his fang grazes over my earlobe.

I explode in an effervescent fuzzy starlight, pulsing up my core. The wave of ecstasy prickles my skin from my scalp to my toes, and I can't control my body as it shakes and my vision narrows.

I'm on the edge of blacking out when the tentacles slide out of me, and I feel Kitaico's fingers weave through my hair.

"You're such a good mate, you're so beautiful, you're..." he rattles on my accolades, and I lie boneless in his arms.

He's kissing my eyelids when I regain my grip on reality. I blink as his muffled voice rings in my ears.

"What did you say?" I mutter.

"I'm sorry I didn't last very long. Next time will be better, I promise," he apologizes for his supposed lack of performance.

"If you're any better next time, I might die…death by orgasm," I laugh, chuffed at what my obituary would read.

He doesn't say anything, just holds me all the tighter.

29 /

second timers

LENA HAS BEEN SLUMPED over me in slumber for some time now. Long enough that her shifting has caused my spent cock to stir back to life.

I don't want to wake her, but I need her. I need my mate.

Maybe my body has created a heat on its own, despite Lena's lack of venom. Or is it knowing now how she feels like a miracle when she's wrapped around me? That I'll never be able to hold another thought in my head besides how beautiful she is when my cock is slamming deep?

Either way, I'm a goner.

I cradle the base of her skull with one hand, while putting my other around her ass, the pert globes of it still slick with our combined juices.

Rolling us both to our sides, I lay her down gently onto her back. Peeling away from her sticky skin, I stand. She doesn't stir much in her sleep, just turning her face into the sheets.

Despite my quick finish, it seems I've left Lena boneless in bliss. Pride blooms in my chest, knowing that I've satisfied my mate, and I stare down at her blushed red body adoringly.

She licks her lips, mewling some sleepy noises, wiggling down against the mattress.

My hand drifts down to my cock of its own accord, and I give it a squeeze as I let my eyes linger over her cunt. The purple of my cum still drips from between her lips.

Don't let it go to waste, some primal part of my brain screams.

Using the hand not pumping my needy shaft, I scoop up my seed and plug it back into her. Lena's delicious muscles flutter as I do.

"Ki-Kitaico?" She lifts her head drowsily from the bed, staring down at me from between her breasts. "What are you doing?" She moans, bearing her hips down against my hand.

"Keeping my seed in, so it roots deep," I tell her truthfully.

She blinks several times, narrowing her eyes between my legs, watching me as I work myself.

"Is that all?" Her brow raises as a sleepy smirk crosses her lips.

"Of course," I assure her hastily. "I would never, not without your consent, I—"

"Take what you need from me. You've been such a good boy you deserve it," she drawls playfully.

"But you're tired," I tell her, still unable to stop jerking myself off as I look at the vision laying before me.

"So give me good dreams," she says before flopping back on the bed.

The trust she has for me with her body makes my heart want to burst from my chest.

Removing my fingers from her entrance, I'm not too distraught with anything that drips out, knowing I'm about to fill her full of me again so soon.

I kneel on the bed, still pumping my hands up and down my shaft, and use my other fingers to spread her delicate little lips.

When my tongue descends onto her pearl, her breath catches, but she doesn't open her eyes.

I suck the little pleasure center, the taste of both of us on her skin creating a heady cocktail that has my cock leaking. When I switch to lapping roughly against the bundle of nerves, her legs clamp around my ears. Looking up over her mound, I see that she's still shutting her eyes, feigning sleep.

This is a game, I realize. I'll play along with anything that lets me lick her perfect cunt.

Letting her pearl slip from my lips with a pop, I sit up, palming the entirety of her now throbbing sex.

"If my sweet mate were awake, she might be able to boss me around," I say haughtily, testing my limits with a smirk. "But since she's just so tired, maybe I'll have to take the reins."

I swear I hear a groan as she grinds into the heel of my hand—it sends a thrill through me. Moving both my hands to her knees, I spread her wide and pull her over my folded legs. Sliding her calves up my thighs gives me the perfect viewing angle of her cunt.

I push my cock down from my belly and use its precum-covered tip to swirl wet circles around Lena's pearl. I know her greedy channel is clasping around nothing from the way she works her hips.

"Do you want to milk my cock, mate?" I ask as I dip the tip just low enough to rest at her soaked entrance. It slips in more than I intend and a "sleeping'"Lena moans at the same moment I do.

I am strong, though, and enjoy the teasing of my mate too much to give into my own pleasure just yet. I pull back my thick shaft before quickly slapping its length down her slit.

To my delight, her eyes shoot open, but only for a second.

"Maybe, if she woke up, she could tell me what she needs," I breathe as I shift my weight. I guide my length back down across her sex, pushing down with my hand, and slide my painfully hard shaft through her slick core.

Each thrust pushes her nub forward, and the pressure of my palm has an ache unfurling at my core. With each stroke, I can feel her tighten beneath me. I'm so enamored with the sight of the head of my cock pushing past her swollen lips that I don't realize the brothers are plucking and massaging her breasts.

I pause my ministrations, thanking the goddess for someone so beautiful, completely overcome at the sight before me.

My neglect must strike a chord, because she finally "wakes up" and our eyes lock.

"Mine to hold, mine to rut, mine to breed, mine to love."

Mine.

I have no control when I push my cock into her tight cunt, thanking the goddess once again that she's been made ready for me already today, not wanting to cause her any pain.

We stare deeply into each other's souls as my hips begin to pump. My mating crest gesticulates against her wet sex, hitting her pearl from every conceivable angle.

"Fuck, I love you," she groans, balling her fists into the bedsheet.

There's an echo of skin on skin as I drive into her. My cock into her cunt, my tentacles over her sensitive nub, the brothers against her nipples.

"I'm so close, I'm so—" She pants as she shatters into stardust under me.

As if on cue, my cock spasms so hard my vision goes black. I'm left in a darkness as I spill into her womb, riding the waves of my orgasm as I slam myself all the deeper into her warmths.

She's shaking when my vision returns, eyes rolled back in her head and mouth agape. I arch over her, kissing her brow and smooth her hair off her damp forehead.

"I would do anything for you—you are mine forever. I love you."

Mine.

☆ epilogue

DAYS TURN into weeks while we help the human women settle into life on the Korlyan Moon. No one seems to have any idea why the despicable Deenz dropped them here, but few of us wish to question it.

For the first time in my entire life, I think females outnumber males. Flocks of human women move through the capital, and the Andjin males can't help but bow as they do.

These females are a blessing from the Great Mother, bringing about the end of the Great Proving.

The emperor, after meeting with the leaders of Sontafrul 6, has officially decreed the Korlyan Moon a safe haven planet for humans. The women are free to leave our moon, even though universal governing senate sanctions won't allow them to go back to Earth.

It seems that many of the males' new Great Proving is convincing these women that they're worth staying for.

The jewels were given the option to remain in their positions or to join the human women. I was surprised at first when not a single jewel stayed in their guarded tower.

It made more sense when Lena explained to me how the freedom to choose your mate, or to not mate at all, would be worth their loss in status.

Two of the jewels even announced a formal life bond. I've heard of males in the temple guard or exiles forming a life bond, but I always assumed it was out of necessity with the lack of females.

"It's shocking that every jewel isn't a lesbian, locked away together for years—not to mention they're hot with their pierced nipples. You're really lucky I didn't run off with Yiskku myself." She closes one eyelid and lets a grin bloom across her face.

I narrow my eyes at her. I've found it hard to adjust to her human sense of humor now that we can understand each other…but the "winks" help. The Andjin are much more literal, and her "sarcasm," as she calls it, has been hard for me to pick up on. But we're working on it, and that's what's important, because inside her womb she carries our young.

As always, the Great Mother has provided.

"I could pierce your nipples if you want," I whisper in her ear as I lean over her, draping her rounded stomach with golden chains, dangling the one with the rough cut emerald over her stomach. The new peaks and curves of her growing body are on full display as we stay naked while in the nest.

"You know, I might take you up on that when they're not so sensitive, after the baby is weaned." She cups her swollen breasts.

"This is one part of human reproduction I have enjoyed thoroughly. One lick of your nipples and you puddle beneath me." I lean over, running my tongue quickly over her breast before she can bat me away.

"You're incorrigible," she chuckles before turning onto her back, stuffing pillows under her strained hips to prop them up, splaying the garlands of gold I've draped all over the bed of our nest.

"Kitaico, we can cool it on the pretty, pretty princess accessorizing, you know. It's not important to me." She pushes one of the chains off her shoulder.

"But it's important to me, to treasure you, to gild you as you deserve…to show you I would do anything to keep you happy," I tell her with a frown.

I'll admit, it's a compulsion to ornament her during our confinement, something left over from the instincts of my ancestors. But it makes me so happy to see her thick with my child, and it feels appropriate to shower these gifts on her.

"What your mate wants is a back rub. Your son is really giving my hips hell today." She sits up halfway, reaching out a hand to me. One of the brothers grabs it before I have the chance and hoists my newly plump mate to sitting.

"I can do a massage," I sigh, bundling up the treasures I've acquired for her off her supple skin. The emerald stone weighs heavily in my hand.

I turn it over. It glints in the light of the glowworms that hang from the ceiling.

This life was once just a fantasy.

I push my disappointment at her rejection of the treasures aside but try to find some compromise.

"Maybe you can just wear this one around your neck?" I hold it up for her with a hopeful smile.

"If it'll make you happy, and I can get you to work on my glutes, I'll do it in a heartbeat." Lena snatches the chain from my hand and throws it over her head before turning onto all fours.

This is a sight I will never tire of. Her heavy belly is too round to lie on, but we've found that this position is a good one. Especially when she opens her hips wide and drops her stomach low.

I grab the shell full of balm—the container has stayed near the bed as we near the end of her pregnancy—and rub a dollop between my hands. I sit, my legs spread wide around hers, and pull her hips back toward my stomach. As I work my thumbs deeply into the socket of her joints, Lena lets out delicious little moans that have my cock hardening quickly.

Another thing I've learned about my mate, besides that fact that sometimes she tells tales for the sake of humor, is that I shouldn't act on my cock's urges until after she is stated with my rubbing of her sore muscles. What I had once assumed was a clever way of enticing me to mate turns out is actually just my mate wanting a different kind relief. It doesn't always mean she won't allow me to take her from behind after her aches are soothed.

So I do my duty, running my oiled hands over the globes of her ass and down her thighs, skirting dangerously close to her cunt as I do. The brothers reach back, wrapping themselves around her puffy feet to constrict some of the swelling away.

"This feels so good," she moans, pushing her hips back further toward me.

I work my thumbs in on either side of her spine and press up to her shoulder blades. She widens her legs as I do, allowing her belly to drop even further down than before, stretching her tight ligaments.

"It's the least I can do for the mother of my children," I say as I rake my fingers gently down her sides.

"Child," she reminds me. Humans don't have litters like the Andjin.

But that's not what I meant.

"When I said children, that's what I meant—I'm going to keep you dripping and full of my seed long after this babe is born," I whisper, feeling her shiver as I stop my hands right near her cunt's pink lips. "Unless that's not what you want?"

With the lightest touch I can muster, I run the tip of my finger along her petals, stopping near her pearl. From this angle, I can see the muscles of her pussy clenching in vain, without a cock to fill it.

"Kitaico…" she pants, lifting her ass back up to me.

"Are you pleased with your massage, then? Shall I work on some deeper muscles, my darling mate?" Cocking my brow, I cup her cunt in my palm.

The brothers fly to their favorite of her assets, kneading her engorged breasts.

"Yes," she responds as her wetness slicks my palm. "I'm yours for the taking, mate."

☆ glossary

☆

The Andjin: Semi-aquatic aliens who live on the Korlyan Moon. Their natural hide is yellow with blue rings but can shift for camouflage. They possess many head tentacles, including two longer ones they use as a second pair of hands called fore-tentacles. Once at war with Sontafrul 6, they now have a fragile peace.

Bukkau: Flying creatures with leathery wings. Large, muscular bodies and large mouths

The Deenz: Hive-minded aliens, traffickers of human women, cheap slimy assholes.

Scripiat: A leviathan-type creature, the size of a blue whale. Bioluminescent whale-shaped head, tail like a stingray/scorpion, the barb at the end glows blue, jagged rows of fangs.

Dredlin: Yellow fish-like creatures

The Fi'len: Semi-aquatic aliens who live on Sontafrul 6. The seven-foot-tall gray-skinned aliens have white hair, four-fingered hands, and four-toed feet. They live in a much more technologically advanced society than the Andjin and are more welcome to outsiders.

Go-Go Juice/Hormone Shot: aphrodisiac shot given to human women by the Deenz before performances.

The Korlyan Moon: The largest moon of Sontafrul 6, home to the Andjin species.

Torun sponges: Purple, a patch near the entrance of Kitaico's nest

Skalpin: Apex predator, tastes like citrus and spice. Dark-blue water snake, lethal teeth, aka "sea dragon"

Worog worms: Purple glowworms, hang from cavern ceiling at the breeding grounds

Security Bubble: Large acrylic oval-shaped bubbles that human women are placed in for their protection.

Universal Governing Senate: The governing system for advanced life forms in the universe. Humans are not considered advanced.

Sontafrul 6: The much larger planet that the Korlyan Moon Orbits. Home to the Fi'len species. A beach planet, frequented by intergalactic tourists.

☆the bubble-verse

All I Wanted Was Sushi But I Got Abducted By Aliens Instead:
Bubble Babes #1

2023

All I Wanted Was To Become A Scientist But Now I've Got An Alien
Boyfriend: Bubble Babes #2

2023

All I Wanted Was a Glass of Vino but an Alien Duke Kidnapped Me
Instead: Bubble Babes #3

2023

Love On The Korlyan Moon

2024

☆coming soon

All I Wanted Was to Read Books but I Became a Space Pirate Instead:
Bubble Babes #4

ESTIMATED PUBLICATION 2024 [PREORDER LIVE NOW]

Soldiers Of Sontafrul 6 #1

ESTIMATED PUBLICATION 2024/2025

☆want more now?

PATREON [https://www.patreon.com/petrapalerno]

I've got some short stories and other bonus content (including very
NSFW art of our lovely couples) on my Patreon! There's also a tier on
where you can vote on a monthly bonus chapter for your favorite
couple!

MERCH SHOP [http://shop.petrapalerno.com]

Signed copies, art, stickers, page overlays, and other fun goodies are available here!